Dillard Ross

The Ukrainian Files

A Series Novel by

Jan R. McDonald

Dillard Ross

The Ukrainian Files

Jan R. McDonald

Published by

Joshua Tree Publishing
• Chicago •
JoshuaTreePublishing.com

13-Digit ISBN Print: 978-1-956823-27-1
13-Digit ISBN eBook: 978-1-956823-28-8

Disclaimer:

Printed in the United States of America

Dedication

To my partner,
Claudia Beverly McDonald

Chapter 1

He looked at the old guy in the mirror and wondered why he couldn't see his reflection. With blue eyes and silver hair, the tanned face stared back at him calmly. He wiped the water from his face, and the reflection did the same. He hated mirrors because they had never learned how to lie.

Dillard Ross finished his morning cleanup and walked back into the bedroom. The one-bedroom condo had plenty of room for his ski equipment and a single suitcase. He had left the skis and poles on the front deck yesterday until they were dry enough to bring in, then he had stowed them in the bedroom. Now he took them back out and put them on the covered deck so they would cool down while he finished dressing for the day.

Dillard would be skiing alone today. His buddy Allan had called off because of twisting his knee the previous day.

That's fine, he thought, putting on his parka. He went out on deck and grabbed the skis and poles. The condo was right on the lift line, so all he had to do was walk a few steps and put on the skis.

Sweitzer Mountain was a nice all-around ski area, not too big, not too small, and for his one-week visit, it was fine. Alan and Sharon lived just a few miles from the resort, and although he was always invited to stay with them, he preferred his solitude.

He slipped the straps of his poles over his gloves, stepped into the bindings on his K-2s, and was set to go. The weather was perfect, upper twenties and clear. The snow would be good, and there were plenty of runs that were not groomed, which was more to his liking. Alan liked the groomed runs, and that's where they skied when together, but Dillard had a free day today, and unless he broke his neck, it would be a good day.

Chapter 2

The news was all about Ukraine and Russia. Dillard had listened to the television for about an hour the previous night then switched it off in frustration. He had visited both countries and liked them both. He had Russian and Ukrainian friends, and it was sad to watch politics hurt both countries. He didn't have a dog in this fight, and he preferred not to pick sides; instead, he hoped there would be a political solution rather than a military one, and soon.

He was sitting by the gas fireplace, looking out at the ski slope, relaxing after a ski day that only resulted in two warnings to slow down. He had declined Sharon's invitation to dinner, promising his availability for the next day. Alan wanted to take the Quad out instead of skiing tomorrow, which, Alan knew, meant drinking beer on some snow-covered logging road. Dillard reminded himself that he only saw Alan and Sharon once a year and that he needed to be gracious and go with the flow. He wasn't sure how many more years Alan would ski—not that it was a physical problem for him, but he seemed to be losing interest in the more physically demanding challenges. He probably saw that old guy in the mirror too, but in his case, he accepted what he saw.

Dillard sat there by the fire, debating whether to turn on the depressing TV news or pour another Jack and Coke, when his cell phone began its irritating sounds. He looked at the caller ID and, after hesitating for a few seconds, answered the call.

A familiar voice said, "We need you to be ready by oh-seven-hundred tomorrow morning. Look for a white van with lettering saying 'PCR Industries,' upper parking lot." The caller hung up.

Dillard put the cell phone down and looked through the large glass window at the pristine white mountain.

I will miss you, he thought.

Chapter 3

Understandably, Sharon was mad when he called and told them he was leaving. Alan didn't say anything, but Dillard thought he was probably relieved. Alan could go back to his normal routine. Dillard promised to stay in touch. He had used the "I have to get back to Florida, something wrong at home" routine. While Sharon did not buy it, she knew she had to accept it. Alan had nothing to say. This wasn't the first time Dillard suddenly had to leave on some emergency, and they knew enough of his history not to ask unnecessary questions. He hung up the phone and went into the bedroom to pack. He'd leave the ski equipment in the condo; the caller would take care of it.

He came back out into the living room, noticing again how comfortable the condo was with its gas fire and pristine view. He couldn't see Lake Ponderay from the front of his condo, but he knew how it must look with the sun starting to set, highlighting the water with multicolored ribbons of light. He would miss this place, at least until he got to another place he liked just as much.

The next morning, Dillard dressed in jeans and a sweater. He had on his hiking boots and figured he'd change into whatever fit the location he was heading to sometime during the travels. He crossed between the cars parked as close as they could get to the ski slope and walked toward the entrance to the parking lot. He saw the white Chevy van idling near the two chemical toilets, available for those skiers that just could not wait. He walked toward it, noticing two men in front, neither of whom he recognized.

When he got close, the driver opened the door and stepped out. He was clean-shaven with dark eyes and dark skin, but unlike Dillard's Florida tan, his coloring was from birth. He motioned to Dillard to go around the van and get in the other side. He said nothing, and Dillard did as he indicated. He opened the right-side door and climbed into the back seat, closing the door behind him. The passenger in front turned to look at him then turned back to look out the windshield. The van started moving out of the lot toward Sand Point. Dillard wasn't surprised that they didn't speak; it was pretty much protocol. He figured the driver and his partner didn't know who he was or why they were picking him up. He noticed that the passenger was armed, a shoulder holster peeking out from his jacket. Again, protocol.

They passed the roundabout and turned toward Interstate 90 / US 95 heading for Spokane. Dillard figured the destination was the airport as he looked out at the white countryside going by. It would take over an hour to reach Spokane, so he settled back in his seat, dozing lightly. He heard a quiet conversation from up front and recognized the language as Hebrew. That knowledge did little to help him figure out where he was headed.

Chapter 4

The Russian Mil Mi-24 helicopter (or, as NATO called it, the Hind gunship) came out of the sun on a mission to cause as much damage as possible. The North Vietnamese had learned American tactics well, and as such, the Hinds were not the easy targets they once had been.

Petty Officer Dillard Ross hid behind a cluster of copperpod trees, directly in line with the approaching gunship. Lt. Rossof lay in the weeds behind a rock outcrop, still bleeding from the hole in his thigh. Dillard checked the M72 LAW portable 66 mm unguided antitank weapon to make sure it was ready. It was a one-shot weapon, and although the Hind wasn't a tank, the M72 should do the trick. It was unguided, but that wouldn't be a problem since he would be standing right in front of it when he fired. He just had to survive the Hind's chin gun autocannon, which wasn't that easy. The turret-mounted, 4-barrel, 12.7 mm Gatling-type machine gun was devastating, and there was little cover. Dillard was betting that he could fire the LAW and dive for cover before they could open fire, but it wasn't a bet many would take.

The Hind was using the sun to hide its approach, but the twin Isotov TV3-117 turbine engines made a tremendous noise, and only its speed made it hard to detect before it was upon you. Dillard knew where the Hind would come from, so even before the thunderous roar of the engines was heard, he was ready. He would have to wait until the Hind was almost on top of him before he could fire. He got himself ready, making sure there were no obstructions or tree roots to trip him up.

Russian Air Force Lieutenant Colonel Boris Sukelov was flying this mission. They had intel that said the Americans were in a camp near Bảo Lộc in the Lâm Đồng province. If they could catch them by surprise, the Hind could do some real damage. The pilot knew he was disobeying orders by flying this sortie, but he was sick of the North Vietnamese and their lack of understanding of what an amazing machine the Mil Mi-24 was. Some people just had to learn by doing, and his North Vietnamese crew and copilot were about to get a lesson firsthand. He hoped it would sink in.

Sukelov backed off the throttles, letting the Mi-24 slow to 160 knots, still fast enough to approach the camp before they could take cover. He smiled, anticipating the havoc he was about to unleash, when a small figure suddenly appeared just in front of the helicopter. Sukelov laughed; the figure was pointing something at the Hind, probably an assault rifle. He ignored the figure, knowing the rifle's fire would do no damage, but he stopped smiling when he saw the vapor trail from the M-72 as it launched its rocket. Too close to evade it, he watched helplessly as the rocket headed toward a spot between the double cockpit of the Hind. He pushed the rudder and collective in an evasive maneuver knowing that it would do no good. The rocket exploded just above Sukelov's head, ripping the blades from the main rotor and forcing the Hind into a steep dive. They were less than one hundred feet off the ground, and impact was almost instantaneous.

Dillard had fired and then dived behind the copperpod trees, covering the lieutenant with his body. He knew that if the Hind crashed near him, they would be dead. Fortunately, they were only hit by the concussion of the blast as the Hind disintegrated in a ball of fire.

"You are one crazy son of a bitch, Dillard," the lieutenant said weakly. "Thank you for saving my life, hell, for saving all of us."

"Just another day at the office, Lieutenant. Besides, I was curious how well the M72 would do against aircraft."

"Tough way to find out, son," the lieutenant said, smiling, then grimaced when he moved his leg.

Chapter 5

They made good time getting to the airport. Dillard was escorted to the TSA precheck and ushered through security without checking his ID or carry-on. The boarding pass the van driver had handed him was for flight 2963 to Atlanta, Georgia, at 11:53 a.m. That gave him roughly fourteen minutes to get to the gate before boarding started. He walked through the airport toward gate A13, debating whether he should grab a sandwich or burger or just keep going. He chose the latter.

When he got to the gate, he heard his name being paged by the girl at the Delta ticket counter. He stood behind a man who had chosen to get his carry-on put into luggage rather than fight for room in the overhead. As usual, he heard the words, "This flight is completely full." Mr. Luggage moved out of the way, and Dillard approached the ticket counter.

"I'm Mr. Ross. You were paging me?"

"Yes, sir, Mr. Ross. May I see your boarding pass please." The ticket agent put out her hand for the pass.

Dillard handed it to her.

"Just one minute please," she said, turning away from him and speaking on her radio. She turned back but didn't say anything as a flight attendant came through the boarding door.

"Mr. Ross, if you would follow me please." She headed back through the boarding door to the plane.

He followed her through and down the ramp to the plane.

The flight to the Hartsfield-Jackson Atlanta International Airport was a little over five hours. Dillard still didn't know why he was going to Atlanta, but someone had gone to a lot of trouble to get him here. Again the special treatment as they held the deplaning passengers until he was off the plane.

As he walked up the ramp, he saw a Navy lieutenant commander standing at the end of the ramp, probably waiting for him. The officer approached him as he walked into the boarding area.

"Mr. Ross, I am Lt. Commander Morris assigned to collect you. If you will follow me please." No attempt was made to shake hands.

Dillard followed behind him as they walked through the busy airport. A gray Ford sedan was waiting at the curb, engine running and a driver behind the wheel. Morris opened the back door, and Dillard got in. He followed quickly, and as soon as the door closed, the driver started out of the Arrivals parking, threading between cars, trying to pick up their passengers. The driver drove carefully, obeying the airport speed rules. Dillard knew there was no great emergency or they would have blasted out of the airport, breaking every speed law. He sat back. Morris was obviously not inclined to have a conversation. Need to know, buddy, need to know.

They turned right off Airport Road onto Interstate 85 and, a mile later, took to the exit for the Airport Loop Road. Dillard had no idea where they were going or, for that matter, why he was there, but he knew worrying about it did no good. He saw signs for Renaissance Concourse Atlanta Airport Hotel and the Delta Flight Museum and guessed he would be meeting whomever at the hotel.

He was wrong. They passed the hotel exit and turned onto Delta Boulevard and headed toward the museum. Dillard didn't know much about it, but the museum was housed in the old Delta hangars from the 1940s. They parked in front of building B. Morris opened the door and got out, holding it open for Dillard.

Without a word, Morris turned and walked to a door marked "Department 914." He opened the door and motioned Dillard in, then he closed it behind him and remained outside. Dillard was a little puzzled why a lieutenant commander would be doing escort duty, but he had learned not to question most government tactics, weird as they were.

This must be the main area for the museum, Dillard thought, staring at an old DC-3 passenger liner from the '30s and '40s. He had actually flown in one in Ecuador in 1998. It had been converted into a cargo plane and was reasonably successful at landing and taking off from the muddy landing strips carved out of the jungles and forests. Still, it was well past its useful life, but in South America, they took what they could get.

Several more aircraft, posters, flight gear, and historical kiosks adorned the museum, and since Dillard was the only person in the building, he took his time walking around and reading the materials.

"Dillard," a voice called out from behind an old Stinson Reliant SR-8E, and he knew the voice at once. It belonged to Lt. Jerry Rossof, someone Dillard hadn't seen for forty years.

Rossof stepped from behind the Reliant wearing a Navy captain's uniform. Dillard assumed he had retired years ago, certainly too old to play ground games with the young bucks. Like Dillard's, Rossof's hair was gray but cut short, military style. He looked trim and healthy as he walked over to Dillard.

"Well, look at you, sailor," Jerry said, eyeing Dillard up and down. "You look like some type of beach bum, all tan and trim." He put his hand out, and Dillard took it.

"We have to stop meeting like this," Dillard said smiling. "People will talk."

"Well, son, we don't want that now, do we?" Jerry always called Dillard *son* for some reason even though they were close to the same age.

"Come on over to the office, and we'll have a little chat." He turned and started walking toward one of the offices surrounding the displays.

All business as usual, Dillard thought, following him.

He went into the office behind him, and Rossof motioned for Dillard to close the door. He sat behind an old metal desk and motioned Dillard to take the only other seat.

"Just so you know, Dillard, I'm a military liaison assigned to Homeland Security now."

Oh boy, Jerry's gone spook on me, Dillard thought.

"Something has come up that I think you can help us with. It has to do with the security of our country—well, that's not really true. The 'security of everyone's country' is more accurate."

Dillard was puzzled. Rossof had never been one for embellished statements, so "security of everyone's country" seemed out of character.

"I know you are aware of the Russian invasion of Ukraine." It was a statement rather than a question. "The US has been doing all it can to support Ukraine, but we can't be directly involved."

Again, not a question. Dillard was starting to wonder where this was going.

"Something has happened over there that could change the Ukraine struggle. Hell, it could even make the threat of a Russian-US nuclear war disappear."

Chapter 6

Dillard wiped the sweat from his forehead with his shirtsleeve. The other men were sweating and swearing in Arabic. He ignored them, pounding another post into the sand and rocks. For the past two weeks, Dillard and a construction crew made up of Canadian mercenaries, plus a group of unhappy Iranian soldiers, were working on a new perimeter fence around the Tabriz Oil Refinery. US and Iranian intelligence services were warning of an Iraq attack on this and several other oil-producing sites in Iran. Both Iranian soldiers and the Canadians had been assigned to Tabriz to help defend the city. Working on the perimeter fence hadn't been mentioned when they signed up.

Dillard had researched Tabriz before being sent here. Like most Arabic countries, Iran has an ancient history that dates back to the Iron Age. Recorded history is always lacking, though, and historians have to look for clues like the epigraph of Assyrian King Sargon II's in 714 BC. Parts of the city are claimed to have been built either at the time of the early Sassanids in the third or fourth century AD, or later in the seventh century.

Looking out at the mountains and Quru River valley sloping down until it was lost on the horizon, Dillard felt regret for the damage that would soon take place. The Iraqis would destroy Iranian industrial and historical sites alike, and that history could never be recovered.

The transport pulled into the compound after satisfying the guards at the gate. Dillard climbed out and headed to his assigned space in the air-conditioned barracks. US Corps of Engineers had built the compound as part of the oil refinery's security, thinking that it might be a target for Iraq. Heavily fortified, the base could house up to eight hundred military personnel and had depot services for heavy equipment and a runway that could support F-4 Phantom jets.

Up to this point, most of the fighting had been further south toward Tehran, but US intelligence warned that Saddam Hussein was launching a new air assault on several major cities including Tabriz. Dillard was there to understand how well Tabriz would fare in such an attack. Iran's oil industry was of significant importance to the United States.

Dillard was awakened by air warning signals. He rolled out of the bunk and quickly dressed, pulling out the small backpack locked in his footlocker. Men were running and shouting in the hallway, just what he didn't need. One question was quickly answered though: the personnel training had been inadequate on what to do in an emergency.

Outside he could see searchlights from the antiaircraft batteries in the compound and in the city itself. At least they were working as they should. He ran over to a parked Iranian Army pickup. Keys were in the ignition. His orders were to take the SAT phone and get close to the Tabriz refinery and report. He ran the danger of being shot by the attacking Iraqis and by the Iranian guards if they saw him steal the pickup, but in the confusion, he should be able to get to the gate without being stopped. Getting past the gate security might be a bit of a problem.

He started the Nissan and turned around, heading for the gate. Dillard drove slowly, trying to look like someone not stealing an Iranian Army truck. He was aware that it would be pretty obvious that he wasn't Iranian Army personnel once he got to the gate, but he'd have to play it by ear.

He was about fifty yards from the security shack. He could see two guards in the shack, both armed. One had turned toward him; the other was still looking out in the opposite direction. No alarm yet. He saw the guard turn and say something to the other man, then both were looking at him. It was too dark to see much detail in the pickup, and his headlights were shining in their face. Dillard figured he had about twenty more feet to go before they could tell he wasn't in uniform.

Unexpectedly, help came from the Iraqis. A burst of explosions lit up the east side of the compound, blowing up sand and rock, but nothing else. The guards ducked, antiaircraft batteries began firing, and Dillard hit the gas, taking out the folding gate. The guards were too stunned to open fire, and he turned his headlights off, racing the Nissan down the road toward the refinery.

Chapter 7

More flashes on both sides of the road gave Dillard just enough light to drive by. He'd gone about fourteen kilometers from the compound, and he'd have to park some distance from the refinery. So far, the attacks were missile strikes. He hadn't seen any sign of mechanized troop movement yet, but that would come. He wondered what the antiaircraft batteries were firing at, maybe trying to shoot down the missiles.

Dillard pulled over and drove into a stand of trees and stopped. He got out, taking his radio and infrared scope. He wasn't armed. Going through the trees, he went to within forty feet of the perimeter fence and, using the trees to screen him, used the scope to check the area. He saw nothing. Dillard wasn't surprised; he figured the Iraqis would just destroy the refinery, not occupy it. What did surprise him was that the refinery wasn't the first target, judging by the missile strikes at the compound. Or was that just a mistake?

He felt the SAT phone vibrate. Someone was trying to reach him. He looked around again, making sure he was still clear, then pressed Receive. Lt. Commander Rossof asked for the status. Dillard assumed he was referring to the refinery.

"No damage yet, sir. Strikes hit near 38.0962° N, 46.2738° E. No known casualties."

"We expect Tabriz is their real target. Tehran, Isfahan, and Shiraz are also reporting attacks. It looks like Hussain wants to damage the major cities and cause as much fear as he can. I don't think the refineries are the targets."

Dillard didn't answer immediately, thinking about Rossof's information. He heard multiple explosions nearer the town. *Looks like they're getting their missiles zeroed in on their real target, the residents of the city*, he thought.

"What do you need from me?" he asked, looking through the nightscope again.

Rossof answered, "We need to know the size of the Iraqi force. We can't get satellite photos because of the clouds, and it's too hot to fly a spotter plane in. You're the only boots on the ground we have in that area."

Dillard thought for a minute. "Okay," he replied, "give me a few minutes."

"Keep your head down, Chief Warrant Officer Ross."

"Roger that," Dillard replied.

Chapter 8

Dillard made good time cutting through the scrub brush and trees. The rocks tried to trip him up several times, but he managed to stay on his feet and keep moving. He had triangulated the missile launches, so he had an idea of what direction to head. Soon he would have to slow down so as not to run into one of their patrols. He stopped behind an outcrop and pulled up the spotter scope. It was still very dark, no moon showing through the clouds. The enhanced image turned the landscape green, but he could tell if someone or something warm-bodied was around by their heat signatures. He saw nothing of interest.

Stowing the scope in the pack, he stood up, bracing himself on the rocks with his right hand. He felt a sharp pain and slapped his hand. A scorpion fell down by his feet, and he smashed it with his boot. He held his hand up and could see the tiny puncture on the back of his hand.

Crap, he thought, sorting through his pack for something to combat the venom. All he had was the Navy's version of an epinephrine auto injector (EpiPen), but that might help. His problem was that he would be traveling, so his blood would be pumping pretty fast. The venom would hit pretty hard, with or without the medicine.

He continued walking toward his goal, his body hypersensitive to the effects of the scorpion. Within minutes from the sting, he was wheezing, his breathing rapid and shallow. He felt waves of dizziness but tried to push through them. Unfortunately, he realized, he wouldn't make it.

Sitting down behind some rocks, he fumbled the SAT radio out from the pack and keyed it. Rossof answered almost at once.

"Sir, I won't be able to report on the Iraqis. A scorpion stung me, and I have to stop traveling. I expect to be offline for about a day," Rossof answered.

"Do you have antivenom?"

"Negative, sir, just an EpiPen."

"Go to ground, ride it out, report back when operational." Rossof was concise and to the point.

Dillard keyed the phone off. He was having trouble putting it away, his muscle starting to tighten. He looked around in the dim light, trying to find a good hiding spot, but it was too dark to see. He gave up, his strength quickly draining away. He sat down at the bottom of the rock, no longer able to stand. His breathing was loud and fast. Not sure how to best deal with the situation, he just relaxed and let the poison do its work.

Chapter 9

illard opened his eyes though he didn't really want to. His hand hurt where the scorpion had stung him, and his arms were covered in a rash. His breathing had slowed, but he had a throbbing headache. He felt weak and wasn't sure if he could stand or if he wanted to try. He tried to reach out for his pack but got dizzy from just moving that much. It was still dark, so he must not have passed out for long. He gathered up his strength and reached out for the pack again. He managed to snag the strap, but the effort of pulling it to him almost made him pass out again. He fumbled the phone out of the pack and, laying it on his leg, pressed the Send button. He could hear Rossof answer, but he was too weak to pick it up. He held the button down and spoke.

"Sir, I'm doing better. It'll take me a few minutes, but I should be able to resume moving towards the Iraqis' location. I must have passed out for a few minutes, but my breathing is better, so I'll be okay."

Rossof replied, "Change in plans, Chief. We have a report that the Iraqis have captured two American doctors who were en route to Tabriz. One of them is a high-value asset, and we need him back. Dr. Rentz is more than just a doctor. Dr. Lee, the female, is expendable."

Ross knew this meant Rentz was probably CIA or some other spook organization. He was still having trouble focusing from the sting, but he did understand what Rossof meant.

"Go find him and figure out how to get him to safety."

But to Dillard, it was a "them," not "him," rescue.

"Where are they now, sir?"

Rossof answered, "Same location the Iraqis were at two days ago when you sent their coordinates."

"Umm, incorrect, sir, I sent the coordinates yesterday."

"Chief, we haven't been able to reach you for sixteen hours. I think that scorpion did more to you than affect your breathing."

Dillard was quiet. He looked around, but there was nothing to show how long he had been unconscious. He just shook his head; he couldn't afford any more accidents.

"Heading out now, sir. Will update at 23:30 Zulu. Ross out."

Chapter 10

Dillard traveled through the scrub and rocks carefully, not knowing exactly where the Iraqis were keeping the prisoners. He assumed they would be picked up and transported back to Iraq for questioning, so it would have to be clear and flat enough to land a helicopter. He was still on uneven ground, but his GPS indicator showed him within two clicks of the longitude and latitude he had transmitted to Rossof. He crossed a small clearing and climbed up a short, steep incline, raising his head slowly to see over the top of the rocks. It was obvious that he had found the place the Iraqis had staged their equipment for the attack on Tabriz. Using his spotter scope, he could tell that the ground flattened out for about a half mile and it had been cleared and trampled down by tanks and artillery. It looked like someplace on the moon with the reduced lighting of the scope. A dirt road came out of the hills to the site then continued east toward the city. It had been used heavily. He saw two vehicles and a portable command tent, but he didn't see any sign of guards. His thermal imager showed only four sources of heat, all inside the tent.

It was too early to call Rossof, so he moved to a spot in the trees closer to the camp. He heard the sounds of the fight in Tabriz, but it was eerily quiet out here. He sat in the trees, watching the tent. He hadn't seen any movement since he arrived. Dillard tried to come up with a plan to retrieve the two Americans. He figured he could take out the two guards, but what then? He had no transportation, and the two vehicles he saw at the camp wouldn't do much good if the Iraqis were here in force. They would have guards on all the roads going in and out of town in case the Iranians tried to counterattack. Taking them out on foot wasn't viable either. They had no equipment, and it wouldn't be hard to track them down. This location was too hot to bring a helo into. He expected the Iraqis would show up within the hour.

Dillard thought for a while and came up with a solution, although he decided not to tell Rossof what he was planning. The lieutenant commander would veto the idea, but Ross knew there was no other choice. Rossof would tell Dillard to get the two doctors and find a place to hide until help arrived. Unfortunately, Dillard knew their chances of survival would be very slim. His was the only way.

He saw movement by the front of the tent. One of the guards had come outside and was talking on a SAT phone. He was looking up, but Ross couldn't see anything above them. Then he heard it, the distinctive turbine whine of the Mil Mi-8. He still couldn't see anything, but the guard turned and went back into the tent. Within minutes, the Russian-made helicopter came in from the west, no lights showing. It hovered about fifty feet above the staging area, probably scanning the area for combatants. Satisfied, the landing lights came on, and it descended to the ground, kicking up a cloud of sand and dirt. Both guards came out of the tent; one was approaching the helicopter, while the other stayed at the tent, probably to guard the prisoners.

Dillard made his move while the dust and noise distracted the guards. He crouched down and quickly crossed the clearing using the tent to block their vision. He approached the side of the tent now ten feet from the front end where the guard was standing. He couldn't see what the other guard or the helicopter crew was doing, but he hoped they were still by the helicopter. Dillard used a small extendable mirror to peek around the front and saw that the guard was turned away from him, watching the helicopter. Being careful not to make noise, Dillard approached the guard and quickly placed his knife under the guard's chin and shoved upward, dragging the already-dead guard backward and into the tent out of sight. He dropped the body and turned to look at the two doctors. Both were bound with mouths taped. He left them that way and quickly went back out of the tent. He now had the guard's assault rifle, but the next steps depended on surprise in order to succeed.

Dillard got lucky. There were only two men on the helicopter, the pilot and copilot. The M-8 was still running, and he saw the copilot climb out and head back toward the tent with the other guard. They were coming to get the two prisoners, but they wouldn't like what they'd find in the tent. He thought about it for a few seconds, deciding to take them as they entered the tent. They'd be surprised for about five seconds, enough time for Dillard to act. He hid on the side of the tent away from the helo. The two men approached quickly, obviously in a hurry to collect the prisoners and leave. He hoped they'd both enter the tent before they saw the dead soldier. He had dragged the body as far back as he could. Dillard got lucky; they both got inside before they realized something was wrong, but that was enough time. He wasn't worried about noise, except gunfire, so again he used his knife to take both men down.

Chapter 11

Dr. Sharon Lee had seen a lot of death here in Iran, but the almost-casual way the man killed the three Iraqis was unnerving. She wasn't sure who she feared more: the captors or the rescuer. The cold blue eyes bothered her even more. He seemed almost bored, and she could tell his breathing and pulse rate weren't elevated. He should be spiking with adrenaline. Just a walk in the park for this guy. She shivered, and not from the cold.

After quickly checking the prisoners, Dillard went back out of the tent and down the side away from the helicopter. This would be the hardest part—approaching the pilot without being seen. He knew he'd have to use the assault rifle to take him out; he'd never get close without being seen. He tried to remember if the side windows of the M-8 were bulletproof, but he didn't think so. Most damage to helicopters came from below, and that was where most of the armor was. He sighted the AK Tabuk at the bottom of the pilot's door then raised the barrel slowly until he was zeroed on his chest. He needed the biggest target he could get that would still disable the target. He took a breath, then let it out, and fired. The result was what he wanted.

Dillard had thought about keeping the pilot alive to fly them out, but he realized the pilot would probably try to crash and kill them rather than be taken prisoner in Iran. Iraqis knew what would happen to a combat prisoner, and he would want to avoid that.

Dillard ran to the M-8 and pulled open the pilot's door. The Iraqi fell out, dead from a pullet through the heart. He turned and ran back to the tent, dropping the Tabuk on the ground. Inside he cut the zip ties on the two prisoners' ankles then their wrists. Last he peeled the tape off their mouths and roughly jerked them to their feet. The woman almost fell, but he caught her and, half dragging, half carrying her, headed out of the tent.

He didn't look back at Rentz; he'd follow or he wouldn't. Dillard was still miffed at the expendable comment by Rossof.

He half dragged, half ran toward the helicopter with Dr. Lee, Rentz right on his heels.

"Get her in the cabin! You take the copilot seat!" Dillard shouted over the noisy engines. This was the first time Dillard had spoken to them.

Leaving Lee with Rentz, he ran around to the pilot's side, almost tripping over the dead pilot. He climbed in and looked at the controls. All the labels were in Arabic, and it was Russian, so the layout was different from anything he had flown before. But some things don't change. The throttles, cyclic, rudders—all the normal controls were the same, so he figured he'd just go for it. What choice did he have?

Chapter 12

Rentz was in the copilot's seat, so Dillard figured now is as good as any time to try this. He knew to keep the tailpipe temperatures from raising too fast by overrevving the engines, but that was the extent of his knowledge about the M-8. He increased the engine's revolutions per minute, and the rotor spun up. He raised the collective and positioned the cyclic to change the rotor angle to about forty degrees. The helo started to lift and spin to the right, but Ross remembered to use the left rudder pedal to counteract the torque rotation. They began to wobble forward, and he increased the collective to gain altitude and steadied the tail rotor with the rudder pedals. Using the cyclic, he nudged the helo forward, still gaining altitude. They were flying.

Dillard had Rentz get the GPS out of his pack and get the coordinates of the nearest friendly camp. They were about forty clicks from the closest friendly. He had the doctor hand him his SAT phone, and he called Rossof.

"Chief, I was getting worried. Status?"

"Forty clicks from Managam in an Iraqi helicopter. Package secure."

Silence for a few minutes, then Rossof said, "Go to the east end of the camp, land near the metal hut on the outside of the fence. Repeat, outside of the fence."

"Roger that, outside of fence. Out." Dillard kept flying toward their destination, wondering who would try to shoot them down first: Iraqis or Iranians.

"Thank you for rescuing us, Mr. . . . ?" Rentz said.

Dillard turned and looked at him. "You're welcome." He turned back to his flying.

Dillard could see the lights of Managam up ahead. Almost as soon as he saw them, they saw him, and he was lit up with searchlights. Threat warning alarms went off, and a computer voice was saying something in Arabic.

Oh boy, he thought, *this is going to be exciting.*

Rentz said, "They do know we're friendly, right?"

Dillard just smiled.

He flew toward the west end of the compound, the searchlights tracking him. He saw the metal building and fence and flared up to land on the outside of it. He had never landed an M-8. Hell, he had never flown an M-8 before, so he expected the landing to be a bit rough. He cut his airspeed down, changed the angle of the helo, and used the cyclic to lower himself to the ground as easily as possible. He figured not getting shot out of the sky was harder than landing, so he should have it made. He glanced back at Dr. Lee, approving the death grip she had on the straps holding her in the cabin seat.

A few seconds later, they touched down or, rather, fell out of the sky. The landing was hard; they bounced back up a few times until Dillard cut the power, and then they stayed down on the ground. Lights still silhouetted the helo, and he could see a dozen or more Iranian soldiers pointing their assault rifles at them.

A Humvee pulled up as he shut the engines down. Two US soldiers jumped out, their assault rifles pointing at Dillard and Dr. Rentz. Rentz didn't look so happy. The soldiers motioned them to get out of the helo; two Iranian soldiers ran up to the cabin door. One opened it, while the other kept his rifle pointed at the cabin opening. Seeing only Dr. Lee, they motioned for her to climb out, lowering their weapons. The two US soldiers lowered theirs also.

The US officer, a major by his insignia, approached Dillard. He looked curiously at his civilian clothes but addressed him respectively.

"Sir, Major Walters, United States Army. Welcome to Managam." Fortunately, he didn't salute because Dillard probably would have laughed and offended him. He certainly didn't know that Dillard was a lowly chief warrant officer.

"Thank you, Major, I'm happy to be here." He shook the major's proffered hand. "If you don't mind, Major, I need to use your communications gear as soon as possible."

"Certainly, sir, if you will follow me."

Chapter 13

Rossof said, sitting back in his chair, "I know you've seen the news from the past few months."

"Yes, sir, I'm aware of the issues, or at least the issues reported in the news."

"Did you know that the US has another big reason why they don't want Russia to occupy Ukraine, besides our relationship with that country? And that other reason has nothing to do with humanitarian efforts or favored nation or any of the other normal reasons we usually quote to justify our involvement."

"Gee, Captain, what a surprise." Dillard knew that the US always had a whole bag of reasons it could pull out to justify whatever it was up to.

"Back off, Master Chief, this is something different, not something the politicians came up with."

"Captain, I haven't been a master chief for over thirty years, and as for the excuses the US uses to make them look . . . um . . . honorable, it doesn't really matter to me. Whatever the US is up to in Ukraine, Captain, I'm not involved in it, nor am I interested in being involved."

He stood up to leave, figuring whatever Rossof had in mind for him, he wouldn't be interested in. Leaving, he opened the door, and faced a man armed with a 9 mm Ruger pointed at his chest. He turned back to face the Navy captain.

"Really, Captain, do you need an audience that bad?"

Rossof just looked at him and pointed at the chair.

"What if I told you we have a way to shorten—no, end the Russian aggression in Ukraine."

"You mean, a way that is different from a nuclear bomb?" he asked Rossof.

"Not funny, Master Chief, and I am dea serious," Rossof said.

"Then I would ask why the US hasn't done what it can do. Why let thousands of Ukrainians die over this senseless war?" Dillard said, his anger rising.

"Because the tool we need is still in Ukraine, and until we get it out and back to the United States, we can't do anything. And this is where you come in." He opened the top drawer and pulled out a laminated box with a thumb drive inside it. He slid it over to Ross.

Ross picked it up, noticing the lettering on the bottom of the box that said "совершенно секретно," which he translated from Russian as "Top Secret." He looked at the drive inside the box, and he could see the same Russian lettering on it.

"What are we doing with a top secret Russian file, and how does that stop the Ukrainian war?" Dillard said.

"It's not what is on the drive that is so important, it's who we got it from. That person is the tool that will end the Ukrainian conflict and maybe even eliminate the threat of a nuclear war."

Chapter 14

Jimmy looked back at the chief warrant officer riding with them. He respected the fact that CWO Ross had made officer the hard way in the Navy, but he still couldn't figure out why a Navy officer was riding in an Army Humvee toward a hot zone, fitted out in combat fatigues, vest, and assault gear. Add the fact that the guy was probably twenty-five years older than the oldest of his squad, and it made even less sense. He looked fit enough, but that might not mean much once they got to the mountains of the Hindu Kush.

Gunnery Sergeant Jimmy Welsh looked back out the passenger door window. They were making suitable time, almost to the start of the Salang Pass, which would take them toward Kabul to the south. US troops hadn't had much trouble with IEDs on this road, probably because it was so heavily traveled by Afghans.

Their orders were to get Mr. CWO to Jalalabad safely and quickly. Welsh had no idea why, or why this Navy guy rated a personal escort through Taliban country, but here they were. So far, the trip had been routine, and intelligence said they were clear all the way to Jalalabad. Trouble was, intelligence was wrong as often as it was right, so they were all on alert.

Corporal Russel, the driver of their Humvee, turned to Jimmy.

"We'll stop before the Salang Tunnel for a piss break. Tell Jeff and Mike to be on alert." Welsh nodded and keyed his radio. Even though Welsh outranked Russel, the corporal tended to take charge of the Humvee when he was driving.

That was okay with Jimmy, and he keyed the radio. Jeff was in the turret, and the only way to talk to him was by onboard radio. He could talk to Mike in the jump seat and the CWO in the back seat.

"Jeff, it's Jimmy. [Of course, Jeff knew it was Jimmy calling. Who else would it be?] We're going to stop before the tunnel for a piss break. You've got lookout, then I'll spell you when I'm done. Out." He didn't wait for an acknowledgment.

Then Jimmy turned around, facing the CWO. "We're going to take a short piss break before the Salang Tunnel. Make it quick."

The CWO didn't seem happy about the stop, but oh well, he was just a guest anyway. He passed the information on to Mike.

They were over eleven thousand feet up, and the air outside was cold and thin. Jimmy stayed in the Humvee until Jeff said it was clear then hopped out, rifle at the ready. He looked around quickly, but there was nothing but rocks and snow. It was deathly quiet except for the wind. He headed over to a piece of granite bigger than their truck and started urinating on it. He heard Mike getting out of the truck, complaining about the cold and snow. Afghanistan, it was either too hot or too cold. Jimmy hated the place. He noticed the CWO hadn't gotten out of the truck.

Probably has prostrate problems from sitting in front of a desk all day and can't pee. He chuckled to himself.

Dillard checked his wrist map against the GPS. They had made suitable time, but this was dangerous territory, and he wished the Army guys took it a little more seriously. At least they had left the turret gunner in place to keep an eye on things. He didn't like where they had stopped. It offered no shelter or protection in case the Taliban was operating nearby. Intelligence reports were usually a day late on their information. He'd also been told that it was clear all the way to Jalalabad, but he dismissed the report as wishful thinking.

He watched Lance Corporal Welsh walk toward the Humvee. Welsh signaled the turret gunner to climb down, rubbing his arms and stomping his feet to keep warm. The driver was still over by the rock. Dillard climbed out of the truck, bringing his pack with him, and started walking over to the boulders. Welsh thought it strange that the CWO had brought his pack with him. They'd only be out of the truck for a few minutes.

Mike unstrapped the turret harness and stood up, starting to get cold without the truck heater running. Something hit him in the chest, sending him over the side of the Humvee. A second later, the report of a large-caliber gun could be heard. Then all hell broke loose.

Chapter 15

Welsh dropped to the ground, as did the other two soldiers. Mike was dead, there was no doubt, realized Jimmy. The high-caliber round had left a gaping hole where it entered and exited. Even from fifty feet away, Dillard could tell that he was beyond help. The trick now was to keep the other three soldiers and himself alive.

They were all blocked from the shooter by the Humvee. It was imperative to get away from the truck, because if the Taliban had handheld rockets or grenade launchers, it was the next target, figured Ross.

"Guys," Ross called out, "get behind these rocks away from the truck. Use the Humvee as a shield. Do it quick."

Mike hesitated, but Jimmy figured out what Ross knew and, crouching down, made his way behind the granite boulders. The corporal and Mike followed. They realized now why the CWO had brought his pack with him.

"If we go into the tunnel, we'll be trapped. Our only way out of this is to pick our way through the rocks and get past them. They'll be expecting us to head for the tunnel. What equipment do we have?"

The soldiers looked embarrassed.

"We left everything in the Humvee, sir," the corporal said, looking embarrassed. "I can sneak back and grab our gear and rifles, only take me a minute."

"No," Dillard said forcefully, "they'll be expecting that. Take out everything in your pockets."

They did as he ordered.

"We have two butane lighters, a penknife, and two rolls of spearmint lifesavers. They'd go in the pack." Dillard had a .45 with two extra clips, a portable GPS, and night vision goggles. "I think there's a flint and steel on my Ka-Bar. Sergeant, would you check it please. The rest of us will keep a lookout."

Jimmy did as the CWO asked and confirmed the contents.

"I expect they left the sniper and someone with a launcher here and the rest went to the tunnel. There must be access to the tunnel someplace not far from the entrance. That's where they'll set up an ambush." Dillard thought for a minute.

"They know that a patrol will come by when HQ realizes we have not checked it. That will be a little while because the tunnel prevents us from radioing, so they don't expect to hear from us for a while. The Taliban know this too, so to them, time is critical also. What they don't know is that my GPS is also a position transmitter, and if we're lucky, someone will realize that we've stopped moving and send a team to investigate. Meanwhile, we have to find a defensible position." He started looking around and noticed an outcrop of granite with boulders blocking two sides. Only the front was open.

"There." He pointed. "We'll have cover from three sides. We just have to be alert in case they try to get to us from above." Dillard started down toward the outcropping, making sure to keep shielded from where he thought the sniper would be. Seconds later, the other men followed him.

Inside the makeshift bivouac, they noticed that they were completely screened except directly in front.

"Mike, take first watch in case they try to route us out. Grab the .45 out of the pack. Remember, we have little ammunition, so don't shoot unless you have a good shot."

"Yes, sir," Mike said, and getting the .45, he headed to the front of the outcropping, keeping himself concealed as best he could.

"So, we need reconnaissance to confirm they're doing what I think they're doing. Also, they'll be in a hurry because of the weather. When the sun goes down, it will drop below freezing, and even the Taliban don't want to freeze to death. Hopefully, a patrol will get here before dark."

"So what can we do, sir?" Jimmy asked.

"Are either of you trained in mountaineering?" Dillard asked.

Jimmy and the corporal looked at each other, both shaking their heads no.

"What about Mike?" Dillard asked.

Again they shook their head no.

Dillard sighed. "Okay, looks like I'm elected. When I leave, keep your eyes peeled in case they get tired of waiting. If they don't hear gunfire from inside the tunnel in about thirty minutes, they'll probably come looking for us here."

He took his night vision goggles and his Ka-Bar and crawled to the entrance where Mike was on watch. He explained what they were doing. Mike didn't seem to like the plan, but he had no choice.

"I'm going around the rocks to where I can start climbing up to the top of the tunnel. Keep an eye out."

"Yes, sir," he replied.

Dillard started scrambling over the rocks, away from the truck and tunnel entrance.

Chapter 16

The CWO had been gone for about twenty minutes. Mike was getting restless, convincing himself that the sniper had fled. If that was correct, they could make their way back to the Humvee, signal the CWO to come back, and drive themselves out of there. He had read that the Taliban liked to do quick strikes, then they'd disappear. He figured that's what they had done. He didn't know anything about the CWO and had no reason to think he knew more than they did. He left his post and crawled in to talk to the sergeant and corporal.

The ground was frozen, a light dusting of snow covering the rocks. Dillard took his time; twisting an ankle would be the last thing he needed. One good result of the cold was that the rocks were frozen in place, so his climbing was quiet. The mountain was mostly dry grass and rocks with a few straggly trees trying to stay alive. It was slippery, but his boots held a good purchase, so he kept going up. He could tell the air was thin, besides being cold, and he tried not to overexert himself to keep his breathing slow. Still, it was hard going, and he could tell he wasn't twenty anymore.

About four hundred yards from the crest, he stopped by one of the straggly trees to rest. He'd need all his energy for what was coming next. Just then he heard a tremendous explosion.

There goes the Humvee, he knew. He wasn't really surprised. These guys didn't know him, and he figured they had convinced themselves that the truck was safe to approach. He hoped they weren't all dead.

Dillard reached the crest and slowly raised his head, trying to match the movement of the grass in the wind. He could see nothing but rocks. He knew better than to get in a hurry. The Taliban knew their business, so he shouldn't expect them to jump up and say, "Here I am." He slowly pulled the scope up to his eyes and scanned the area about one hundred yards away. There! Something seemed out of place, although he couldn't quite tell. He kept the scope focused on that spot. Sure enough, the spot moved a few inches. That was all he needed. He still couldn't tell if it was one person or two. Certainly, one person could be both sniper and launcher. On the other hand, the Taliban had enough followers to use two men to do this job. The real question was, Did the ambush party in the tunnel hear the explosion, and was it on its way back?

He started sliding over the rocks on his stomach. He used every outcropping and rock to conceal himself, but it was more a matter of luck than anything else if he made it to them undetected. He hoped the shooter still had on his ear protectors.

Dillard got within fifty feet and stopped. He could see the shooter clearly, and there was only one. The launcher lay next to him as he scanned below with the sniper scope. His ear protectors were still in place. Dillard made the fifty-foot run in record time, plunging the Ka-Bar into the shooter's neck before he could move.

But resources were scarce because of the refugees fleeing from the city, so outside help had been drafted to help build the fence. All that would change once the Iraqis attacked, which, ironically, the men hoped would be soon. They were more comfortable with a Norinco CQ or Sayad 5.56 assault rifle rather than a shovel, so there was a lot of grumbling, which Dillard ignored. The crew figured he was a mercenary like the Canadians, so there was no undue interest in him.

They finished the last post. Another crew would stretch the metal fence and razor wire, so the men were finished for the day. They'd find out their assignments back at the camp tonight. Dillard climbed into the US Army transport, and it rumbled off toward the city. The men were hot and tired, most of them not used to the physical nature of their assignment. Hoping for a job that let them stand around holding their rifles, they were looking forward to a reassignment. Dillard knew that since they had been assigned to Tabriz, they weren't on anyone's A-list. He wondered how they would do if Iraq did attack the refinery.

Chapter 17

The C-130 Hercules arrived at Boryspil International Airport at 1:00 a.m., Eastern European Time. The airport was empty. Civilian airlines had stopped travel to Ukraine, and it had been declared a no-fly zone. The Ukraine Air Force was headquartered in Vinnytsia, some 263 kilometers from Kiev.

Dillard Ross was the only passenger on board the transport plane. He stepped out into the frigid wind, his eyes watering. Two vehicles waited for him on the tarmac, a Chevy Blazer and a Mitsubishi Montero. He walked toward the Montero, knowing that although it was slower than the Blazer, it was built like a tank and was reliable. Where he was going, he couldn't afford any kind of breakdown. No one had come out of the vehicles, so Dillard just walked over to the Montero, pulled open the back door, and got it. His bags would follow later.

Inside the car, it was warm, too warm. He rolled down the window, and the driver turned around to look at him.

"Sir, my instructions are to drive you to Vinnytsia. You will be staying at the Hotel France. Tomorrow morning, you will be picked up by Dr. Evans and taken to the site. I'm sure Captain Rossof explained that Dr. Evans is in charge of the Vinnytsia site and that you are here to help with security. The Russian missile attack completely destroyed the Vinnytsia airport, but the Ukrainians took it back.

"The Russians have moved on and are not attacking Kiev from the east, but we never know when they might decide to move in on Kiev from the southwest, which will put Vinnytsia right in their path. We're hoping to finish our debrief and transfer the asset to the United States. Until we are ready, we have to find some way to protect it from both the Russians and the Ukrainians. Neither government is aware of what we are doing or who we have, and we are working hard to keep it that way. At some point, someone will find out. Dr. Evans and her team are the experts we need to verify all this risk is worthwhile. You just need to keep them safe while they figure it out, then get the asset out unharmed."

The Montero headed out of the airport, the Blazer following close behind. He could hear muffled explosions from the direction of Kiev, so the fighting must be fierce.

Such a shame, he thought.

Outside the white landscape whirled by. They were making decent time, and the only real slowdowns were the small towns they passed through. Dillard knew their progress was being monitored by satellite, which was also watching out for both Ukrainian and Russian forces. The Ukrainians weren't aware of the US involvement at the site; they thought it was just an international archaeological dig with NATO guards, fairly common in Ukraine even during a war. Scientists tended to ignore the outside world. It would be hard to explain Dillard's purpose here if the Ukrainians stopped them. The Russians would just blow them up, no questions.

They had traveled 125 kilometers to the site. Medzhybizh and Berdychiv were both crowded, but Vinnytsia was only another 80 kilometers, and they made good time. Not everyone was willing to drive the highway with the war going on, so they met little traffic.

The SUVs pulled into the hotel parking lot. The driver of the Blazer got out and went in, and Dillard and his driver waited in the Mitsubishi. After a few minutes, the soldier came back out and approached the truck. Dillard rolled down his window.

"Sir, you are in room 104. Here is your room key, no need to stop at the desk. Your bag will be delivered shortly. Captain left something for you on the table when you go in."

Dillard thanked him and his driver, got out, and went inside.

The Hotel France Vinnytsia was on the main street in the heart of town. It was a stone building with a lobby, pool, and exercise room. The suites included a sitting room and views of the downtown area.

Dillard let himself into the suite. It was one of their upgraded rooms with a mini fridge and a balcony facing the street. Stylishly furnished, it was European in style with comfortable upholstered chairs and a heavy wood table. Internet connection ports were in the bedroom and sitting room.

On the table was a bag with a note attached. It read:

Enjoy this. You're gonna need it.

Regards,
R

Inside the bag was a six-pack of Coke and a bottle of Jack Daniel's.

Chapter 18

Dr. Evans, or rather one of her assistants, introduced himself to Dillard in the lobby. Introductions done, they headed outside to the waiting Toyota Land Cruiser, and Dillard got in the back seat. A woman with dark hair and light complexion was sitting in the passenger seat, and she turned to him when his door closed.

"Mr. Ross, I'm Dr. Lee Evans, the leader of this project. You may as well know that I was not in favor of having you here. This is a CIA endeavor, and I can't see how one person can be effective in protecting us from two armies." She took a breath, trying not to get too worked up.

"My team and I are more than capable of getting the asset out of the country. Our government, who arranged this meeting, has insisted that your presence is necessary. I have no idea why. We've had no security issues, and I don't expect any, at least not the kind that you would be involved in. What I am saying is that I may have to put up with your presence, but understand, I am in charge of this asset, you are merely the hired help. Stay out of our way, don't ask questions about things that don't concern you, and we'll do okay. Do you understand me, Mr. Ross?"

Dillard was quiet for a moment, then he said, "I have a question, Dr. Evans."

She looked perplexed then said, "What is it?"

"Have you lost any team members in the last two weeks?"

"What the hell does that matter? Maybe you didn't understand what I told you earlier." She looked at him angrily.

"Oh, I understand what you said, and I have no problem with it, but I need you to answer my question." She thought about making a smart remark but noticed how serious he looked. She decided to answer him instead.

"Tim Porter, our so-called cryptographer, went to town a few weeks ago and didn't come back. One of the other crew members said he wasn't happy with the project and he probably flew home. I wasn't too worried about it. He was a low-level agent. Why?"

"Just background information, Dr. Evans. Was Mr. Porter on your team long?"

"Well, no, he was one of the newer members from our German intelligence group. He had impeccable credentials and was particularly good at what he does. Everyone liked him."

"Thank you, Doctor. I have no other questions."

Dr. Evans looked at him for a moment then turned around. *Strange man*, she thought.

She was expecting some gung ho Marine type with too much testosterone and too few brains. Dillard Ross didn't match that expectation. His hair was gray, and from a distance, she figured he was in his fifties. Now up close, she wasn't sure of his age because his face was completely unlined, unlike most men of fifty, but his manner was respectful, and she hoped he would stay that way.

There is something different about him. She wasn't sure what. *Maybe it was the blue eyes and tan skin or his corded forearms, but he radiated something,* she thought. *Was it pent-up violence? No, something else.* Then she had it. *Confidence, he radiated confidence.*

She was a little embarrassed about how forceful she had spoken to him. Fortunately, it didn't seem to faze him at all. She'd ask Tom, their CIA security chief, to find out more about Mr. Dillard Ross. Tom would be reporting to Ross, but she knew Tom would still take his orders from her. Dillard Ross didn't need to know that. After all, he didn't work for the CIA.

They pulled into the gated lot where the team parked their vehicles. The gate was staffed by two armed men in nondescript jumpsuits wearing NATO armbands. Dillard knew that NATO knew nothing of this project, so that was just for show. They parked the Toyota next to Tom's Jeep and got out, locking the car behind them.

Chapter 19

The dig site was a mound of dirt ten meters high and two hundred meters long. Like the Scythian burial site found near the city of Dnipro, archaeologists had found the signs of a prehistoric Indo-Iran culture about twenty feet down from the surface and evidence of a more recent culture, having been built around the fourth century BC, near the top. However, it was whom they had in residence here, not the ancient artifacts that got Dr. Evan's team put in place.

Steel double doors had been framed and built into the mound, which was where they were headed. Dillard followed the driver and Dr. Evans to the doors, noticing that it had a keypad, not a normal-locking doorknob setup. The driver of the Toyota keyed in a code, and the click of the locks was audible.

Seven characters, Dillard's mind subconsciously filed the information.

The doors swung outward, not inward, so they stepped back to allow them to open. Inside it looked dark, even though lights were set in the framed walls and turned on. Coming in from the direct sunlight, it took a few seconds to get used to the subdued lighting, especially when the doors closed. There was humidity, something Dillard was surprised about. He had assumed it would be dry under the mound. Acclimatized, they continued down a long corridor of rock and dirt walls. Braces were attached at four-foot intervals to keep the earth and rocks from moving.

After about thirty feet, Dillard started seeing what looked like the remains of ancient rock walls, which seemed to have been partially excavated. This was probably as far as the first archaeologists got. He remembered the briefing saying that the entrance to a solid rock tunnel was found near an ancient Scythian rock wall. No, it said, "found under a Scythian rock wall." They walked a little farther and stopped.

To their right, part of the rock wall had been taken down, and a small shed was where it had stood. He guessed the entrance to the tunnel must be inside the shed. A man was clearing debris from the wall, carefully looking at each rock before he put it in a basket to be stored or disposed of. He didn't stop working as they walked up.

A light was coming toward them from the path past the shed. It bounced around, so Dillard figured it was a lamp attached to a helmet. As the light got closer, he could make out a man about six feet tall, wearing a miner's helmet and jumpsuit with a NATO armband like the men at the gate. He walked up to Dr. Evans and stopped, never taking his eyes off Ross.

"Dr. Evans, glad to have you back, ma'am. I assume this is Mr. Ross," he said, putting out his hand to Dillard.

"Tom Lansard. Mr. Ross, a pleasure to meet you. I've heard good things about you from Captain Rossof." He smiled.

Dillard took his hand, and they shook.

"Thank you, Mr. Lansard, I've heard good things about you too. Perhaps we can talk after our little tour, and you can bring me up to speed on your security procedures. And by the way, my name is Dillard."

"Be happy to, sir—I mean, Dillard."

Formalities finished, Dillard turned his attention back to Dr. Evans.

"When the first archaeologists were here, they accidentally knocked down part of the rock wall by dislodging a boulder up there on that shelf." She pointed to a hill rising up and away from the wall. "The boulder rolled down and knocked out this part of the wall. When they were cleaning up the debris, a hole was found where a cornerstone used to be. They widened the hole until they could see down into what looked like a cavern of solid rock. The rock walls of the cavern had been blasted out and reinforced by someone years before. The tunnel, its existence unknown until recently, ran several miles beneath the Ukrainian countryside and came out in a town called Dvorichna, which had a train station where the trains ran all the way to Moscow."

"Whom was this reported to, Dr. Evans?" Dillard asked.

"Only the intelligence team here and their contact in the UK knew of the asset."

"What triggered the US government's involvement?" he asked.

"One of our agents in Russia got word that there was an unofficial manhunt underway for a person of major interest to the Kremlin."

"Where was the initial contact done?" he asked her.

"Here, and before you ask me, anyone who knew of or even suspected the identity of this man is now a guest of the US somewhere safe."

Chapter 20

Dillard Ross pushed off from the beach and paddled through the Bahia grass. He knew the bass and bluegill hung out in the grass so they could hide and strike when something swam, floated, or sank near them. Dillard didn't really care if he caught any fish. It was the process that he enjoyed. Still, a nice bass or bluegill fillet would be a nice dinner, but he wasn't getting his hopes up. As a kid growing up next to a river, he had been an avid trout fisherman, but fishing here was a little different. Still, the calm water under clear blue skies was hard to beat.

He paddled for a while, heading for a pile of deadfall that was half in and half out of the lake. He just knew a big lunker was lurking under the waterlogged trees. Gliding up, he dropped his homemade anchor over the side and came to a stop. He thought about getting a Stella Artois out of the cooler and popping it open, but he decided not to, maybe later. For now he'd just sit here, play with his crank bait, and hope for the best.

The cell phone in his windbreaker started vibrating.

No way am I going to answer that, he thought to himself. He didn't.

Instead, he cast out again, trying to get as close to the trees as he could without snagging them. He reeled in, and wham, a strike about thirty feet out. He set the hook and started reeling it in. He was surprised at how hard it fought. Must be a decent-size bluegill.

The fish broke out of the water, its silver skin flashing in the sun.

That's no bluegill. That's a bass, and a good one, he thought.

He let out a little whoop, then the fight was on. The fish kept trying to turn back to the sunken trees, and he had to tighten the drag to keep it from peeling the line off and snagging him up. It surfaced again, and this time he got a good look at it. That fish must be over five pounds. Wow! He was really into it now, slowly reeling him to the kayak, enjoying the struggle. The fish actually pulled the kayak, and his anchor came loose several times, but then it caught and held. Tiring, the fish was slacking off, getting closer and closer to the boat. He had it about five feet from the hull when he bent down to get his net. He held the pole up, keeping pressure on the fish as he used his left hand to put the net in the water so he could drag the fish toward it. With one more giant effort, the bass rolled over, shook its head, and dislodged the lure. With a flash of its tail, it was gone. Dillard just sat there for a minute then smiled happily.

He did pop a beer open, part in celebration, part in tribute to the one that got away. He sat there and drank the beer, content to be on the water with no schedules or missions to think about.

If this is what retired folks do, I should have retired long ago, he mused.

Finishing the beer, he put the empty can in his cooler and picked up the paddle. He pulled up the anchor and set it in the back of the kayak, turned the kayak, and headed back to the beach. On the way back, he tried to decide whether he wanted to barbecue something or go to town to Harry's and have dinner. But that was an easy decision—crab-crusted redfish royale on a bed of smashed garlic potatoes on Harry's outside patio. Of course, he'd order the Louisiana Fondeaux as a starter.

He loved the place and its location in St. Augustine at the start of the old town. Even though he rarely went down there to the shops and old forts, just knowing it was there and the incredible history of the oldest city in the United States made dinner at Harry's that much more pleasurable.

Funny, he thought. Most of his life he had tried to avoid meeting people because of his job. Personal associations and emotional ties were not encouraged, so his life had been one-night stands or short relationships. His record during the past ten years was about a weeklong affair. He no longer had to go by those rules; the problem was that he had no idea how to do anything but hit and run.

Even though it was a weekday and summer vacations hadn't started yet, he was standing in line, waiting to be seated at Harry's. He didn't mind. It had been many years since he had felt so relaxed, and he was kinda getting into watching the people in line and passing. He couldn't stop himself from analyzing everyone, so he just made a game of it.

Okay, he thought. *The guy four people ahead of me with the good-looking blond is not married to her. He has a ring, she doesn't. Cheating? No, don't think so. I can see no guilt on his face. The woman, a looker, is relaxed, friendly, and having a good time. They're friends, maybe even family*, he thought. *Now that's different*. Still smiling, he turned to look behind him at the others standing in line. Three women were in line, talking and laughing, enjoying their night out. One of them had dark hair and skin, probably Hispanic, and she was smiling and staring straight at him. *Busted,* he thought and turned back around.

He asked for a patio table when it was his turn. The hostess almost frowned, seeing that he was alone and she'd have to waste a whole table on him. She shrugged—not her problem. Besides, it was Thursday, not their busiest day, and there was still plenty of room. His server came up to lead him to the table. Young guy, probably a college student. He chatted amiably, and Dillard realized he didn't have to say anything; the young guy was on a roll. Seated, he ordered a Jack and Coke and looked around.

Harry's usually had a local musician in the evening. Dillard was glad to see a microphone and a guitar were standing back by the wall, waiting for the music hour, which was usually about 7:00 p.m., ten minutes from now. Several tables were still empty, but that wouldn't last. His drink arrived, and he ordered Louisiana Fondeaux, relaxing. A man, his wife, and his son were brought to the table on his right.

Probably vacationers, he thought, noticing their red skin from the Florida sun, but they looked like they were having a good time.

He took a sip of his drink and watched his waiter escort the three women he had noticed to the empty table on his left. Just like with him, the server led them to the table and was having a conversation with himself as they were seated. They ordered drinks and an appetizer, and he disappeared to reel in the next batch of diners. A street-weary Floridian shuffled across the patio and up to the microphone, picking up the guitar. Dillard knew not to judge before he heard them sing and play. He had made that mistake before.

"Good evening, folks. I'm Randy Forester, and tonight, I'm going to make your drinks a little sweeter and your food a little more delicious. Y'all have a good time tonight." There was a light smattering of applause, and Randy started strumming and singing.

After his first song, the crowd was mesmerized. As he had experienced before, this guy, who looked like he lived on the street, could sing and play as well as anyone Dillard had heard on the radio or television. He knew the people seated on the patio would be wondering why someone with the talent Randy Forester had was playing in a restaurant and not making albums or television appearances.

He watched the drinks for the ladies come, and soon after, his dinner arrived. A few minutes later, he noticed approvingly that they had ordered Louisiana Fondeaux as an appetizer. He smiled to himself then noticed that the dark-haired woman was staring at him again. She probably thought the smile was for her. Was it?

She was certainly attractive enough, probably in her late forties or early fifties, and very well-preserved. She wore a minimum of makeup, and her dark skin and dark eyes were set off by her cream-colored dress. Not flashy, but as he looked around at the other diners, her looks had drawn more than just his attention.

So what's next? he wondered.

He thought his gray hair would have garnered disinterest from someone like her, but apparently not. She was looking at him again, and her friends had started to notice her interest. The three talked quietly to one another, smiling and glancing at him occasionally. Their food had come, and Randy was on his third song. For a few minutes, they, and he, focused on the food and the music.

Randy's first set was finished, and he put his guitar down to the loud applause of an appreciative audience. He thanked everyone and walked across the patio to take a break. Several people had gone up and put money in his tip jar, and Dillard knew there would be much more before the night was done. He had finished his dinner and drink and signaled for the waiter.

"So what dessert would you like tonight?" the waiter said with a smile. "I personally recommend the key lime pie. I think it's the best in St. Augustine. Shall I order that up for you?"

"No, but thanks. Just the check please," he said, watching the server's smile dip just slightly. "And something else. I wish to pay for that table also." He nodded at the table with the three women. "How can I do that?"

"Easy, sir, just order another drink or two, and when they are finished, I'll have the total for you."

"Won't do. I'm going to leave now. Do you have an idea what their tab will be?"

He thought for a minute then pulled out their ticket. "Well, the dinners and appetizers ran about $99. They each had a cocktail, and they'll probably order another. I'm guessing about $125 without tip."

Dillard thought for a minute. "Tell you what, I'll give you $175. If it is more than that, the difference is on them. If it's less, the difference is yours." Dillard knew the server would still try to hit them up for the tip. "Oh, and another thing, I don't want them to know who paid for their meal. Got it?"

He paid both bills and got up to leave. The dark-haired woman saw him get up and smiled, probably thinking he was coming over to introduce himself. Her two friends were watching expectantly. He smiled at her and turned to go out the patio door.

Chapter 21

Dillard left the restaurant and walked south on Avenida Menendez. He crossed over to the harbor and looked out at the sailboats and motorboats anchored on both sides of the Bridge of Lions. Traffic was fierce, like always, in downtown St. Augustine, but he ignored it, turning his back to the street. It was a warm night, a common occurrence in Florida. The temperature had dropped to about seventy degrees, and a breeze carried the smell of brine and fish off the water. He loved it.

Dillard stood there, leaning on the walkway railing, when he felt a touch on his shoulder. He turned and was face-to-face with the pretty Hispanic woman from the restaurant.

"What you did in the restaurant was very nice," she said. "I wanted to thank you in person, but you had disappeared." She smiled shyly.

"I'm not very good socially," he said, smiling back.

"So now I have to ask, why did you buy us dinner? You didn't come over and introduce yourself, so it wasn't because you wanted to get to know any of us better." She stopped talking, waiting for his explanation.

Dillard cleared his throat and said, "Uhh, well, I guess it was just nice seeing three attractive women having a nice time together. Simple as that."

"Simple as that? Do you know how unusual that is around here?"

"Not really," he said. "I don't get out that much, so I'm probably not up on today's social etiquette. It just seemed the right thing to do, and I can afford it, so why not? If it made your evening a little nicer, then I'm pleased." He turned back to look out at the harbor, thinking their conversation was over.

To his surprise, she turned to look at the harbor also, standing next to him at the railing. Neither spoke for some time.

She broke the silence and, turning to him, said, "My name is Gabriele Larson. I live here in St. Augustine. I work for Flagler College in their

Admissions Department. I'm a widow and have two grown children that live in nearby towns. I haven't been on a date for over a year, and this is the first time in months I've been in town past 9:00 p.m."

She put out her hand, and Dillard shook it.

"Your turn."

He looked at her. "Dillard Ross, retired Navy. I live in Keystone Heights on a lake. I've never been married, and every few weeks, I come to town for dinner at Harry's. I've spent most of my life away from the US, and now I'm trying to figure out how to blend in, and I don't have a clue." He suddenly realized he was still holding her hand and quickly let go.

"I wondered if I was going to get that back," she laughed. "Well, Mr. Ross, you've just made a new friend. I don't meet many well-mannered single men that don't have secret agendas. I need to get home, but I hope I'll see you again?"

Dillard realized that was a question, not a statement. "It's Dillard, Gabriele, and I have a question. Do you like boats?"

Chapter 22

Who has been in contact with this man?" he asked.

Dr. Evans thought for a moment then answered, "Tom Lansard, myself, Myrna and Jim, my field agents, and Terry and Yossif from the original contact team."

"No one else? What about the agent that left?"

"He'd have no reason to . . . uhh . . . Wait, I think he went with Tom one time for something. He might have seen him, although I doubt it."

Dillard frowned. "Okay, I'll talk to Tom." He turned away and looked down into the dark cavern. "Thank you for your hospitality, Doctor. If you don't mind, could you have someone show me to my quarters?"

She was surprised. She thought he would demand to go down into the interrogation room right away, and she was prepared to fight him on it. His job didn't require him to be down in that area, not until she was through with her validation. She just couldn't figure him out.

"Rollie, would you show Mr. Ross to his quarters please?"

Rollie, he saw, was the man who was categorizing the fence rocks. Dillard turned to follow Rollie, then he turned back.

"Tom, could we get together tomorrow about 7:00 a.m.? I'd like you to bring me up to speed on any security issues."

"Sure, Mr.—I mean, Dillard. We'll have breakfast while we go over the details. Rollie will collect you and bring you to the cafeteria."

Rollie took Dillard to his room, which was spacious compared to many accommodations he had used in the past. The walls were covered with a thin material rather than just bare rock, but the absence of windows was obvious. He saw that his bags had been delivered, and he opened the smallest one.

Inside there was a SAT phone wrapped in his underwear. He didn't expect it to work under the mound, but he would try anyway. No signal. He put it back. Next he took out a small camera called a GoPro. It was housed in a headband that fit on his ballcap. He set it aside. Next he pulled out a flashlight and put it beside the camera. Last his Ka-Bar in its belt scabbard. He got out his cargo pants and a heavy plaid shirt. He'd wear the SWAT boots that he'd bought online.

Rollie had shown him the communal bathroom with its rows of sinks and walled shower stalls. He'd grab a quick shower then lie down. He planned to be up by 2:00 a.m. for the other part of his tour.

Dillard's Fitbit alarm sounded quietly. He swung his legs off the cot and slid his boots on. He loved the zippers on the boots, which eliminated tying laces. He was already dressed, preferring to sleep in his clothes rather than having to dress when he got up. He stood and opened the door quietly. He had already checked that the door didn't squeak before he went to bed. He peered down the dark tunnel that led toward the interrogation room and holding cell. Quietly, he headed out, making sure nobody else was up. He made it to the main tunnel and turned toward the rooms. It was only one hundred yards to the locked room and cell, and he quickly unlocked the door with a pic. Opening it, he left his flashlight off, making sure nobody was inside. He saw no lights, so he started in, being careful not to trip on anything. He turned on the GoPro.

There was a raised hospital bed in the center of the room that had restraints bolted to the frame. On a table were two voice recorders and a video camera with a microphone on a stand. A monitor and PC were connected to the camera, probably for editing and packaging to send electronically. Other than those few items, the room was bare.

He crossed the room to another locked door. This one probably went into the holding cell. He didn't want to alarm the guest, so he wouldn't try to go in there. He just needed a quick look at the facility and what equipment the CIA had set up for the interrogation. As Rossof's brief had said, the setup of the interrogation room was pretty much standard. Walking back to the computer, Dillard placed a device on the back of it near the audio/video ports. He knew that intelligence officers, especially integrators, were so focused on their work that they ignored their own security measures. Tom was the only one Dillard was cautious about.

He moved across the room until he got to the doorway. He opened it slowly, scanning the tunnel to make sure no one was about. He turned the

GoPro off and quietly went out the door, locking it behind him. He looked at his Fitbit. He'd been inside for about fifteen minutes.

Chapter 23

As promised, Rollie was waiting at his door at 7:00 a.m. He followed him down the hall to the cafeteria. Tom was seated at one of the four tables; the other three were empty. He said good morning and pointed at the coffee maker on the counter by the refrigerator. Dillard walked over to it, put in a pod, and pushed the blinking Start button on top. The Nespresso coffee maker whirled and hummed and spit a frothy concoction into his cup. He picked it up and carried it over to the table, sitting down across Lansard.

Dillard took a sip and was surprised at how good the coffee was. He looked at Tom and said, "Give me a rundown on the security setup, including the guards at the gate."

"Well," he said, "the front guards are not NATO personnel, and neither am I. We wear the armbands to look authentic. It's not unusual to have NATO security and international archeologists at a dig around here. I have three other men assigned: Rollie, the two men at the gate, and myself. Our mission is mostly to observe and report anything unusual to Dr. Evans. Now that you are here, we will report our findings to you."

"Where did you come from, and how did you get assigned here?" he asked Tom.

"We are all field agents, but we were ordered to leave all personal identifiers at the base in Kiev. That's where we met Agent—I mean, Dr. Evans."

"What do you know about the project here?"

"Rollie and I know that a high-profile defector or informant is being questioned here, and the circumstances lead me to believe that he is someone of high interest to the US. We don't know his identity, but we know he is Russian. The puzzle is Dr. Evan's presence. She is not a field agent, and I'm guessing that she's pretty high up on the food chain in the agency. Why would they send a non-field operator to a war zone, and why are they keeping information from us, the agents on-site? Dr. Evans is a big liability if something goes wrong and the Russians try to take Mr. X back. I'm sure she knows things that we don't want the Russians or, for that matter, the Ukrainians to know. Is that why you're here, Dillard, to make sure she doesn't fall into the wrong hands?"

Dillard didn't answer. "Have any of the other security team members been inside the interrogation room?" Dillard asked instead.

"No, Rollie is stationed up in the main tunnel, clearing and cataloging debris from the Scythian burial site to keep our presence legit. The other two men have never been near the room or the cell."

"Okay, then the only loose end we have is the agent that left the team, correct?"

"Uh, yes, sir, that is correct. When he didn't show up, I asked Captain Rossof to try and find him, but he was unsuccessful," Tom said.

Actually, Dillard knew that wasn't correct. Rossof had found the agent; he just didn't tell Tom about it. Porter was found dead in an Iranian hotel in Tehran. Why he was in Iran and with whom he was meeting was the real question and one of the main reasons Dillard was here in Ukraine.

"Any surveillance equipment set up? I saw the one video camera by the entrance. Anything else deployed?" he asked Lansard.

"That camera's all we have installed. Do you think we might need to upgrade our detection equipment?"

"I do, Tom. I'm here because there is concern that information about whom we have here may have been compromised. We're not really in a position to add security personnel. It would draw too much attention from the Ukrainians, so we'll have to make do with the staff we have now. However, I did take the liberty of ordering more detection equipment, and it should get here today. I'm hoping that will be enough to give us time to call in help if we need it."

"I see, so your expertise is counterespionage?"

"Among other things, yes." Dillard finished his coffee and stood up, ending the conversation. He turned to leave then turned back to face Tom. "I'm afraid you won't get the information about me that you were after. I assume Dr. Evans requested you to do it?"

Tom looked embarrassed and just nodded his head yes.

"Don't worry about it, I would have done the same thing." He smiled and walked away.

Dillard went out the front entrance. He had been given the code for the door so he could come and go. He would have them change the code daily from now on. He walked out through the parking lot toward the shack. The two guards watched him walk up.

"Dillard Ross, gentlemen," he said when he was close to them. "Did Tom brief you on my involvement?"

"Yes, sir," both responded nervously.

Dillard knew they were borrowed from the air base and probably had no clue why they were there.

"Relax, guys, and it's not *sir*, it's *Dillard*."

Both looked more comfortable after he said that. No telling what they had been told about his being there, especially since no one here knew why he was there. Tom now believed he was some kind of surveillance expert sent to beef up their detection systems. Not too far off track, and it would do.

"So you know, I'm here to upgrade your surveillance systems. It seems the site might be getting more attention than we like. I'll do my work and be out of your hair as soon as possible. Meanwhile, we'll probably make a few changes, like rotating shifts out here at the gate. I'll include Rollie and Tom in the rotation so nobody will be stuck here every night, okay?"

They both nodded yes.

"I'm going to take a walk around the dig now to get familiar with the area. Anything special I should know about?"

"No, sir," both men responded.

"Remember, it's *Dillard*, not *sir*. You men have a good day." He walked out the open gate and turned right to walk the perimeter of the mound.

The access road had been cleared about twelve feet away from the trees. It ran all the way around the mound in a big circle until it intersected with the road coming in. It was in decent shape, the surface mostly sand, but it had been packed down when the road was built. Dillard didn't think the rains would wash it out. That was the good news. The bad news was how much cover surrounded the site. Other than the roads, the surrounding ground was thick with trees and rocks, hilly with steep gullies. He'd have to neutralize the threat it represented.

He completed circling the mound and walked away from the site down the access road. He walked about a half mile and stopped, looking at both sides of the road, planning his defenses. As soon as Rossof had told him about Porter being found dead, he knew it was a matter of time before they started getting unwanted visitors. How that would occur, he didn't know, but it was his job to plan for unforeseen contingencies. He looked around again and turned to walk back to the site. Going past the gate, he waved at the two soldiers and let himself into the dig through the two doors.

Chapter 24

Just like he said, an unmarked truck pulled up to the gate. The guards checked their papers and directed them where to park. Dillard had Tom ask the guards to come and help them unload the truck. Tom had shown him one of the empty rooms some distance away from the dig site that they could use for storage and whatever else Dillard needed it for.

Tom was surprised at the large quantity of boxes in the truck. There were even several desks and cabinets.

This guy must believe there is a real threat, he thought to himself. *I don't think he's telling me the whole story.* He sighed and helped one of the guards unload a desk.

They carried it into the room, Dillard pointing to where he would like it set up. The rest of the unloading went about the same way, Dillard pointing out where he wanted stuff stacked or set up. He had asked Tom a lot of questions about power, backup power, food stocks, etc. He made it sound like they would be under siege, but Tom just answered him, thinking he was being paranoid. He said nothing.

Dillard didn't ask them to open the boxes; he'd do that himself. He knew he was making them wonder what was going on with all this stuff, but it couldn't be helped. Hopefully, it would turn out that he was just being paranoid. He figured that's what they thought anyway, and they may be right.

Unloading over, the transport left. Dillard asked that the gate be kept down at all times unless they were letting someone in. He knew the pole gate wouldn't stop anyone trying to come in, but it would at least look like they were alert. He also knew that there were mixed feelings about the rotating shifts at the guardhouse. Too bad it was necessary.

Meanwhile, Dr. Evans and her team had spent the day in the interrogation room. He was curious about what they had accomplished and what they thought of his being here. Later he would connect to the listener he'd put on the PC. He had no visuals, but the audio would do fine.

At about 6:00 p.m., the whole crew except for the duty guard assembled in the cafeteria for dinner. Dillard learned that the crew took turns fixing dinner, which was a series of microwave meals heated up and plated. He had eaten much worse. There was an unspoken rule about no alcohol, which he appreciated; but there was a whole list of juices available and powdered milk, which he couldn't stand. He was one of the last people to arrive, and there was only one seat open, and it was next to Dr. Evans.

Boy, this is staged, he thought and walked over to her table.

"Please sit, Mr. Ross," she said smiling. Obviously, his last night's visit hadn't been discovered, or there would have been fireworks. "I hope you had a good day. I'm sure Tom has assured you that our security is fine?"

"I have no complaints, Dr. Evans," he said, smiling back. "Tom has been a great help. And how was your day?"

"We had a fairly good day. Myrna is trying to research some of the information we collected. Mr. Ross, I'm not an idiot. I'm sure you were briefed on what we know found so far?"

"Yes, ma'am," he said. "Dr. Evans, may I ask you a question?"

She hesitated, then reluctantly nodded her head yes.

"Were you able to verify our guest's identity?"

She frowned. "I guess you have been briefed." She sighed. "No, Mr. Ross, we were unable to verify our guest's claim. We're still working on it. Right now the DNA testing is the holdup." The conversation with Dr. Evans stalled at that point.

Tom asked him if he had been in the military.

He said, "Yes, thirty years."

"Visit any interesting places while you served, Dillard?" he asked.

"Depends on what you think is interesting, Tom. Vietnam was interesting, so were Iran and Afghanistan. There were several more places that I visited that were interesting, but I guess I'm just a natural tourist. I find most places interesting." He smiled and turned away.

Chapter 25

For the next three days, Dillard busied himself unpacking and listing the equipment. He tagged Rollie to help him wire in the display monitors that interfaced with the new surveillance cameras. The two desks that were set up became monitor stations. With this equipment, he could see all sides of the mound, front to back, side to side. Several of the camera units had thermal imaging and infrared sensors. He set alarms for heat signatures, movement, and sound. He had decided not to use ATR (or automated target recognition) software because he had no idea what their threat would be. With the systems he installed, it would be very difficult to get within half a mile of the site without triggering an alarm. Dillard even mounted two cameras on the top of the mound pointing up at the sky.

He had a display put in the guard shack that also showed all sides of the site and half a mile of the road to the entrance. With Rollie's help, he ran wires down the tunnel to the cafeteria and to the shed. An audible broadcaster was placed in each location, but they were not enabled. That would happen only if they were under attack.

The last installs of their defense perimeter he would do alone. These weren't more cameras; they were weapons, and he was afraid they would cause too much concern if some of the team members knew about them, especially Dr. Evans. He had decades of experience with weaponized perimeters, both offensive and defensive experience. He had a pretty good idea of what they could and could not achieve. It wasn't the best scenario.

It took him two more days, but he finished his defenses just before their supper hour. Apparently, Dr. Evans and her team still had not been able to verify the guest's identity, which confused him since almost everyone was in a database of some sort and the CIA had great resources to find it. Photographic materials wouldn't work since it was relatively easy to change someone's looks. They had also taken a DNA sample, but they must not have the results back yet. He'd try to probe her a bit more, but he didn't want to upset her.

As usual, the seat next to Dr. Evans—or Lee, as she now allowed him to call her—was open. He collected his micro-dinner and juice and headed over to her table. They all greeted him, and he returned it and sat down. He could feel the air of disappointment, so he simply said, "No luck with the guest, huh?"

"I'm at my wits' end. He doesn't want to talk to us until he is on US soil. I need to confirm his identity, either by DNA or from the information he gives us." She chuckled nervously.

Okay, here it goes, he thought.

"Listen, Lee, I know I'm just a security guy and don't have your technical expertise, but I have been in almost every part of the world, and I've seen a lot of guests. If you will allow it, I'll go into the interrogation room with you tomorrow and see if I can see something you didn't." He expected a quick rebuttal.

"You know, Dr. Evans, he might have an idea that we haven't thought of," Myrna said.

"Yes," said Tom. "Maybe he could help."

She still looked unconvinced, but sighing, she said, "Okay, but if he does decide to talk, you will have to leave. I know you have a high-security clearance, but his information is ultrasensitive, and I am not willing to share that responsibility with anyone but the director himself."

"Understood," he said and started eating his meal.

At 7:00 a.m., he made his way to the cafeteria, poured coffee, and nuked an egg-and-bacon sandwich. He wasn't convinced it was real egg, and the bacon was questionable, but he figured he might miss lunch, so this would hold him for the day.

Rollie was there. Tom came in a few minutes later. None of the interrogation team showed up.

"What time are we going to the room?" he asked Tom.

Taking a drink of his coffee, he replied, "My guess is that Dr. Evans and her team are already in the room awaiting your arrival. You know she just wants to prove you wrong, don't you?"

"Yeah, the thought crossed my mind when she gave in so easily, but that's okay. Chances are, she's right."

They continued eating and finished up, put their disposables in the bag, and headed out to the interrogation room entrance. Sure enough, Dillard saw a little gathering of agency geniuses waiting for them.

"Sorry, Tom, as far as you go today," Dr. Evans said. "Mr. Ross, if you will follow me please." She turned and opened the door.

Uh-oh, he thought, *back to* Mr. Ross *again. Bad sign.*

He walked inside and looked around. They had turned on the lights, and it was bright with the wall reflections. He waited for someone to tell him where to sit, but they ignored him. Myrna and Dr. Evans walked over to the door of the cell and unlocked it. When it opened, Dillard saw that the cell was actually a small room with a bed, a dresser, a video player, and a TV.

So the guest hadn't been treated too badly, he thought.

They didn't go into the room; rather, they waited for him to come out. A man in his midthirties walked into the room. He was dressed in jeans and a hooded sweatshirt and wore no restraints.

Interesting, thought Dillard. The man appeared gym-fit but was starting to soften from lack of exercise. He looked at Dillard with a guarded expression, not sure if this new guy was a good or bad thing. He walked over to the conference table and sat down. Dillard walked over and sat across from him.

Dillard knew his name was Yarslova, or Ярослав in Russian. He used the Russian pronunciation and greeted him in his own language. Yarslova responded in English.

"Yarslova, my name is Dillard, and I am here to make sure you and Dr. Evans get back to the US safely."

He watched his reaction, then Yarslova spoke to him in English.

"I know who you are, Mr. Ross," he said smiling. "Your normal tasks are usually more violent than this situation warrants—that is, unless you think Russia knows I am here. If that is the case, even your exceptional skills will not save us."

"And what do you know about my exceptional skills?"

"You must remember that my father was an intelligence officer before he rose through the ranks in Russia. I had access to much of the intelligence regarding foreign agents. Although you were not considered an intelligence operative, there was a lengthy file on you dating back to Vietnam. You made very interesting reading, Mr. Ross, almost like those superheroes Americans are so fond of."

"I think a lot of what you read about me must have been made up. I'm certainly not a hero of any kind." Dillard shook his head. "And regardless of what you read, I'm just here to get you safely to the US." Dillard thought for a minute and decided not to ask Yarslova any questions.

Dillard stood up and turned away from Yarslova and looked at Dr. Evans. She was surprised at how quickly he had terminated the conversation with Yarslova. He didn't even try to get any information from him.

"I'm going back to check on Tom. Let me know how your research goes." What he meant was, "Let me know when you confirm his identity." He turned back to Yarslova and said, "It was good meeting you, Yarslova. I hope your conversations with Dr. Evans are beneficial to both of us."

Chapter 26

Dillard was in the cafeteria when Dr. Evans came it. Her face was red, and she looked angry.

"Rollie, Tom, would you leave us please, and shut the door behind you." It wasn't a suggestion; it was an order.

Both men got up and hurried out. When she heard the door close, she looked down at Dillard, who was still seated at the table, pulled something out of her lab coat pocket, and threw an object on the table. It was his listener from the computer.

"This is BS!" she shouted at him. "I'm going to call Deputy Director Brad Jensen right now and get you removed from this project." She grabbed the SAT phone and angrily started dialing. She reached Jensen after two rings.

"Sir, I just found a listening device planted on our computer by Dillard Ross. I want him removed from—"

Suddenly, a different voice was on the phone.

"This is US Navy Captain Rossof, Dr. Evans. How may I help you?"

"Why are you on this line? I was talking to Deputy Director Jensen from the Central Intelligence Agency and now—"

Rossof cut her off. "I'm sorry, Dr. Evans, but Mr. Jensen is no longer in charge of your efforts in Vinnytsia. I have been assigned by President Freemont to replace him. Mr. Jensen will be calling you on your SAT phone to confirm this as soon as we are finished. Dr. Evans, this project is no longer an intelligence-gathering exercise. It has been elevated to immediate extraction. You will be taking direction from Dillard Ross until you are on US soil. Is that clear, Dr. Evans?"

She began to sputter, "But . . . but . . . this is an intelligence event, and you're not even CIA." She almost cried. "Dillard Ross is not cleared to

"

run this operation, nor do I believe that you are. Do you have any idea how important this asset is to the United States?"

Another voice was suddenly on the line with Rossof.

"Dr. Evans, do you recognize my voice?" he said to her. "Authentication lima, lima, foxtrot, alpha 4, 9, 4. Please confirm." Evans looked at her electronic NoteTimer to verify the authentication code and appeared stunned, Dillard thought.

Then she responded, "Confirmed, Mr. Director."

"The president of the United States has authorized Captain Rossof, US Homeland Security, and Retired Chief Warrant Officer Dillard Ross to control and implement the extraction of Yarslova Putin from Vinnytsia, Ukraine, to the United States in any fashion they believed necessary. You will remain under their command until the asset is placed in a secure facility on US soil." He sighed. "I also need to inform you that information as to the whereabouts of this asset has been communicated to Russian intelligence by Agent Porter, and they are, at this very moment, making immediate plans to acquire the asset from your location. You are all in grave danger, Dr. Evans. Please do whatever Chief Ross and Captain Rossof instruct you to do."

The line went dead.

She sat there staring at the SAT phone. Dillard felt bad, but it had to happen. He just wished it could have been a little less of a disaster. He knew she was a professional—you don't get that high in the CIA unless you have some serious skills. Like it or not, he expected that she would work with him on saving their lives. He was a little miffed at her for not telling him the DNA sample had proven positive. He had found out from Rossof.

The next day, they went into defensive mode. The agents stopped interrogating Yarslova as soon as his identity was confirmed. Now they were focused on figuring out how to get out of Ukraine. They split up tasks.

Tom and Rollie took site defense. They were up to speed on the surveillance setup—all of it except the weapons. That was Dillard's alone. Tom seemed to appreciate the complex setup and the way it was triangulated to cover all aspects of the mound. The rotating shifts were working out okay. There were still times when no one was at the gate shack, but he felt better knowing that when no one was on duty, the equipment was. Dillard also took guard shifts, just to give the others a break.

Dillard and Lee were hatching out a plan to get out of the site if company suddenly arrived. Dillard told her they would send a unit to probe the site first. They would want to make sure they were still here before committing any serious resources. He figured they could handle the first visit, but it would be followed up with some serious resources, and those they could not withstand. Because the Russians were already in Ukraine, mobilizing forces to Vinnytsia would happen quickly and be seen as just part of the Russian-Ukraine war by the rest of the world.

One thing Dillard did not know previously was that a tunnel ran from under their site to a neighboring town that had rail connections to both Russia and Belarus. The tunnel was a leftover from World War II. It ran about 1.8 kilometers, and if they were really lucky, the Russians didn't know about it. They would have to clear the old tunnel access, but it did offer an alternative exit. Of course, if the Russians did know about it, they could use it to assault the site through the back door.

Dillard told Evans about Agent Porter being found dead in Iran and what that meant. They had to assume the information was given to the Russians, and they would stop at nothing to get Yarslova back or kill him to prevent the United States from getting his information. Of course, they would blame the United States for his death if that happened. The only good news was that they wouldn't want anyone else to know the Russian president's son had defected, so they wouldn't involve any of their allies in his retrieval.

Evans just looked at him for a long time. Finally, she said, "Okay, I believe you're telling me the truth. It doesn't sound like we have much of a chance, but let's try to work together on this. I don't know what else to do." She put out her hand, and he shook it.

Chapter 27

Dillard always liked old things that still worked, maybe because he was one also, but somehow the stuff he bought that was a decade or so older seemed to work better, last longer. Case in point was his Four Winns boat. It was really from back in the day, but he had no complaints. It was his third boat, but this one seemed like it fit his needs exactly right. It seated six comfortably and had a reasonable seventy-five-horsepower outboard—which, unfortunately, was a two-stroke, but oh well. It was light enough that he could move it around on its trailer by hand. Like the previous owner, he kept it in his garage, especially since he could lock it up when he was out of town. The reason it was in such good shape was that the family he bought it from kept up the maintenance. Even the transom was solid, unheard of in a boat as old as this one. He hoped she'd like it.

He decided to launch the boat at the Vilano Boat Ramp on the mainland side of the causeway. He'd pick her up at the St. Augustine Municipal Marina. They'd motor up the Matanzas River and on into the Matanzas Bay. They'd stop at Aunt Kate's Restaurant on the North River, and that would pretty much take care of the day. The weather was perfect, light winds and not too hot.

He paid his five-dollar launch fee and removed the hold-downs from the back of the boat and, making sure he had put the plug back in the transom drain, started backing the boat down the ramp. Three feet into the water, he got out and released the bow winch. Using the bow rope, he let the boat drift off the trailer, then climbed onto the walkway, pulled the boat over, and tied the bow and stern. He walked back to the Jeep and drove the trailer out and parked about fifty feet from the launch ramp.

Locking up, he returned to the Four Winns, lowered the motor down to its stops with the electric tilt button, then walked back to the stern of the boat. Under the rear cover were the fuel tanks, and he reached under and squeezed the bulb on the main tank to pressurize the fuel. With that done, he returned to the captain's seat to start the engine. Pushing the key in to choke the motor, he turned the key, and the motor fired up at once. He let it run at a fast idle for a few seconds then lowered the fast-idle lever to a slow idle. He was ready—well, almost. Dillard decided to put up the Bimini top just in case Gabriele didn't like the sun like he did. Five minutes later, he was off.

He made the trip to the marina in ten minutes. As he pulled up to the municipal ramp, he saw her standing at the end. He had described the boat to her, and she recognized it and was waving her arms.

Good sign, he thought. She looked excited.

He idled up to the ramp, cut the engine, and threw her a line. She deftly looped it on a turnbuckle like she was an old pro at this.

"You've done this before, it seems," he said, smiling broadly.

"Mmm, maybe a few times. I grew up on the St. John's River, and my dad had a boat. It wasn't too different from this one actually," she said, looking his boat over closely. "If you're not the first owner, somebody sure took care of this one." She seemed impressed.

Good start, Dillard thought, helping her onto the boat. Gabriele was wearing a light sundress, perfect for what they were doing today. He couldn't help noticing how well she filled it out, and he did like pretty things.

"Dillard, you're staring, and I'm getting embarrassed."

"Sorry," he mumbled and busied himself untying the boat.

"I didn't really mind," she laughed. "Let's hit the water, Captain. I claim shotgun." She sat down on the seat across his.

The day was exceptional. Everything went well—the boat, lunch at Aunt Kate's—and since he had made reservations, they were ushered to their table quickly. During lunch, they shared their histories, but in Dillard's case, his history was toned down considerably. She seemed fascinated with his past and didn't seem to mind his soldiering, which wasn't always the case, he had found. For her part, she seemed to have had a happy childhood. She touched briefly on the passing of her husband, a police officer who was killed in the line of duty. Her children, she said, all had busy lives of their own, and although they all tried to see one another regularly, it didn't always happen. She said she liked being called Grandma, so Dillard knew she was content with her age, which turned out to be forty-nine. She didn't seem to mind that he was older, but if he had been a doddering old man, he doubted that they would be cruising the river right now. She had a lot of energy, which fit his style perfectly.

After lunch, they went back to the boat. It was late afternoon, but the sun was still high. She asked him to put the Bimini top down, another point in her favor. Her dark hair had tiny points of silver that the sun caught when she shook it; otherwise, he wouldn't have seen them.

She said she liked my silver mane, although it is pretty short to be called a mane, he thought.

They were back in Matanzas Bay, across the old fortress Castillo De San Marcos, when she asked him if she could drive the boat. Surprised, he said, "Sure," and moved out of his seat so she could take the wheel.

She smoothly shifted into the forward drive and accelerated to about twelve knots. The bay wasn't the place to speed, and she seemed to know this.

Obviously, he thought, *she's had plenty of practice driving a boat*, as she deftly took them up toward the marina.

He was going to ask her if she wanted him to bring the boat in, but it didn't look like she needed any help as she squared up with the ramp and cut the engine. He jumped out and tied the stern of the boat off, and she went up front and threw him a bowline. Snugged up, he helped her climb out of the bow. Now it was awkward. He didn't know what to say next, and she figured that out pretty quickly. She took a step closer and put her hand on his arm.

"Listen, I know we just met, and I know I want to see you again, and I hope you feel the same way."

Dillard started to say something, but she stopped him.

"Neither of us expected this, so let's just go with the flow. We're not desperate teenagers, so we have as much time as we want to see what does or does not happen. I have no expectations, and I'll be happy with whatever this turns out to be. Is that okay with you? Oh, you can speak now." She laughed.

Dillard smiled at her. "Yes to all the above." He reached in and kissed her.

Chapter 28

D r. Evans told Dillard that they had cleared the opening to the old tunnel and put a ladder down to it. She said the tunnel looked clear, only a few collapses, and they could easily walk it. She didn't know if it was clear all the way. Dillard said he'd send Rollie to explore. Suddenly, a loud wailing started up. Tom was in the control room and had flipped the switch on the alarm, the sound filling the tunnels and rooms.

Dillard got to his feet quickly. "We have company," he told her.

They made their way back to the security room. Rollie was waiting by the door, and as soon as Dillard appeared, he started briefing him. Mike had been on duty at the gate when the proximity sensor went off.

"We saw two trucks with no markings, and both stopped about thirty meters from the gate," Rollie said. "Tom thinks they're troop carriers."

"Has Tom radioed Rossof yet?"

"Yes, sir, as soon as the alert was received. He was asked to get you as soon as possible."

"Okay, Rollie, let's go. Dr. Evans, would you and the other team members wait in the cafeteria while I try to find out what is going on? I'll let you know as soon as I can." He turned and followed Rollie to the control room.

Tom was sitting in front of the monitors, watching the trucks. Both Dave and Mike were in the room also. Dillard took a quick look over Tom's shoulder then started issuing orders.

"Dave, you went to sniper school. I want you to get the .50-caliber out of that cabinet and go up on top of the mound."

Dave did as he was told, not asking how Dillard knew about his schooling. He opened the cabinet, which Dillard had unlocked when he came in, and got the sniper rifle and extra clips of ammunition.

"Sir, I'll go out the door to the right and climb the mound from the back. They'll probably see me come out, but they won't know where I'm going for sure."

"Take a radio and the EMF gun. If you see a drone launch from the trucks, hit it with the EMF. That will disable it. Make sure you aren't on the radio when you fire it."

"Yes, sir," and he was gone.

"Why are they just sitting there? I would think they'd try to use surprise for their approach," Tom said.

"Normally, yes, but they really don't know what we have here, and I'm sure they don't want a firefight that will attract the Ukrainians. Right now they're trying to figure out how to get into the mound without attracting too much attention. I expect Dave will be radioing us about men approaching from the flank. The trucks are a decoy to distract us. They let the men out before we picked the trucks up on camera."

Just then, Dave radioed, "I have eleven men approaching us from the rear. I've moved over behind the cooling vent, but my back is exposed to the trucks."

"Don't worry about the trucks, focus on the approaching men. Can you see any uniforms?"

"Civilian clothes, sir."

"Try to figure out if one of them is giving orders. I want you to take him out when they are even with the scrub pine I painted an orange stripe on. Do you see the tree?"

"Yes, sir, will do." Dave's radio went silent.

"Mike, I'd like you to take out the AK-74 and four clips of ammo and go about one hundred feet past the guard shack and find cover. I want you facing the trucks, but do not open fire."

Mike did so.

"Rollie, arm yourself with an assault rifle and pistol and just wait here. Tom, call the Ukrainian city manager and tell him we will be doing some blasting on the mound for the next few hours."

Tom looked at him.

"Now please."

Tom started dialing. When Tom had made the call, Dillard told him that he and Rollie were going outside for a few minutes, and to watch the screens and let him know if anything changes. Dillard grabbed a radio, a small box with two toggle switches and a push button, from inside the cabinet. He stuck a .45 in the back of his pants and put two clips in his pocket. He wasn't expecting a firefight.

"Let's go, Rollie. Tom, use the intercom and tell Dr. Evans and her team that everything is under control and that we have radioed for help." He turned and went out of the room, Rollie close behind.

"Dave, Dillard here. What is the location of the approaching men? Over."

"They seem to have stopped. They're about fifty feet from the marked tree. Over."

"Good. When they start moving, let me know when they reach the tree. Out."

Dillard and Rollie went out the front door, but instead of heading to the road, they turned right and went along the perimeter road to where it turned to circle the mound. Dillard motioned for Rollie to follow him, and he went into the brush and rocks, found a good place to sit, and started waiting. He knew the men attacking them were having trouble with their communications because he had triggered the signal jammer. It also meant they couldn't call out either, but Ross's local band radios still worked.

The radio suddenly came alive.

"Starting to move, sir. Marked tree in sixty seconds. Over."

"Take your man out, Dave. I'll hear the report. Just stay behind the stack. I have a surprise for them. Out."

A minute later, Dillard heard the bark of the .50-caliber. He flipped the left toggle on the switch box then pressed the momentary switch. The explosions were loud. They went off one after the other in two-second intervals. After two minutes, Dillard radioed Dave.

"Status. Over."

He heard coughing as Dave caught his breath and spoke, "Jesus C . . . Sorry, sir. I can see only four men still moving around. What the hell did you explode? Uh, sorry, sir, I'm a little shaken. Over."

"Four moving targets, Dave. Get it done. Out." He switched channels on the radio.

"Mike, Dillard. Over."

"Yes, sir. Over."

"I want you to start firing at the trucks. Aim for the windscreens, one shot every five seconds until all of your ammunition is gone. Then come back into the mound, meet in the security room. Out."

"Dave, is cleanup finished? Over."

"Yes, sir. Over."

"Come back to the mound, meet in the security room. Out. Come on, Rollie, we're done here."

Chapter 29

Gabriele sipped on her white wine. Dillard was out on the lake at his house, paddling the kayak from bank to bank. She was just enjoying the show. She sighed contentedly. Who would have known that life would take a turn like this? She was resigned to go on as she had: work, home, dinner, TV or bed, then work, home, TV or book. then bed . . . She was okay with that and the infrequent dinners out with the girls and infrequent kid visits, except for the grandbaby-sitting. It wasn't a bad life, but now it was so much better.

Dillard steered the kayak onto the beach in front of his house. He looked happy. *There is a beautiful woman sitting in one of my beach chairs. Guess I'd better go see if she is lost or something*, he thought. He climbed out of the kayak, stretching.

My god, Gabriele thought, watching his muscles ripple. *I can't imagine what he was like twenty years ago.* She smiled happily.

He looked at her, thinking, *My god, what a beauty. I can't imagine what she was like ten years ago.* He smiled happily.

"Let's go up to the house and figure out how to waste the rest of this beautiful day."

"Oh, we'll think of something," she said, smiling mischievously.

After dropping Gabriele off, he returned home. They had talked about having one house, but for now, they had agreed to leave things as they were. It wasn't that they didn't think the relationship would last; it was logistics.

If she came his way, she would be too remote to babysit the grandbabies, and she wouldn't ask Dillard to leave his lake. So for now, things would stay as they were. Her kids loved him, but she expected that. Much as he claimed not to have good social skills, he charmed them immediately, and the grandbabies—wow, she had to fight for their attention when he was around. Brian, her son-in-law, was sold after going out fishing a couple of times. Her daughters thought he was a dreamboat. Funny how life is.

Dillard fixed Frito pie for dinner, and since he was the only one in the house, he didn't have to worry about bean farts. He poured a Jack and Coke and sat down to see what was on Netflix or Prime. Some movie he had never heard of was on, but Tom Hanks was in it, so it would probably be good. The story was about some guy back in the day that went around reading the news to the townsfolk. Who could come up with an idea like that? One thing he did not do was watch war movies. He'd seen too much of that in real life.

At nine thirty, he turned the TV off and went out on deck. He thought about having another drink, but one was his normal limit on weekdays. He decided to pass on the cocktail. Outside the night was cooling down. His screened porch was waiting for him, so he went in and closed the door to keep the mosquitoes out. He was surprised; they had not been a problem like he thought they would since he lived on a lake. He sat there, lost in thought. Outside the owls hooted at each other, and the sandhill cranes warbled. All was well until his cell phone rang.

* * *

"But you are retired, Dillard, they can't make you go anywhere," Gabrielle said angrily. She knew some of the anger was because she wanted him around so bad, and that was selfish.

"Unfortunately, the problem they have is one only I can help with," he said, only half truthfully.

"Oh, give me a break. Ukraine? Come on, Dillard, you can't tell me that there aren't men, and younger men at that, who can do whatever the hell this Rosenberg needs."

"It's Rossof, and if he called me, then he has no other viable options. I'd be last on his list, so he must be desperate. I'm just going to be an adviser. I'm not carrying a rifle or hiking through enemy territory. The part of Ukraine I'm going to isn't even important to the Russians." As soon as he said that, he knew that he blew it.

"Don't bullshit me, Dillard. I read. I know about the Russian attack on their airport."

"Then you also know that it was just stupid and the Russians aren't even near there anymore. Trust me, I'm done being shot at."

Their first fight went on for about another hour. Gabriele knew she couldn't win, but she wanted him to know how angry she was about him leaving. For his part, lying to her was the worst thing he had ever done. They said their goodbyes, arms around each other, making promises both intended to keep.

Chapter 30

Dillard asked Dr. Evans to join them in the security room. He talked about what had just happened, but he left out the details to spare her. What they all wanted to know was who they were and what would happen next. He said the men were probably Russian, men sent after Porter had told them about Yarslova. He said he expected the next visit to be more violent, so he was taking measures to derail more unwanted visitors.

He and Rossof had talked about the situation, and Rossof came up with a good plan, one that might work. As part of the Ukrainian support package from the United States, they would build a temporary training camp on the road to the site. The US presence would deter any more attempts unless they decided just to bomb the mound to dust. But for that contingency, the Israelis had parked two F-16s at the Vinnytsia airport. It would also deter the Russians from any more missile strikes. The planes were there for enforcing the agreed no-fly zone to protect the civilian residents of the surrounding towns. Russia had agreed to this. But Dillard knew that none of their preparations would stop the Russians if they decided to move a couple of battalions to Vinnytsia. He expected that's exactly what they would do. The stakes were too high.

He concluded the meeting by asking Dr. Evans to watch Yarslova and get him and her team ready to move quickly if they were forced to. She said she and her agents would be ready.

Chapter 31

The call ended, and Gabriele hung up the kitchen phone. She sighed, not happy about the situation. Captain Rossof had called, like he did every Thursday evening, to let her know that Dillard was fine. As much as she wanted to hear that, it frustrated her that he would say nothing about what Dillard was doing or when he was coming home. She had no choice but to accept what he told her.

Supposedly, he was working with NATO on an architectural find in Vinnytsia, Ukraine, one that was so important that even a war wasn't allowed to interrupt the project. Of course, he said nothing about this being involved with Homeland Security, which she was probably not supposed to know, or why Dr. Evans, who was supposed to be leading the project, had a doctor of science degree in psychology and worked for the Central Intelligence Agency. It would be hard to explain to her why someone with a psychology degree was involved with an architectural dig six thousand miles from the US. The less Gabriele knew about Vinnytsia, the better.

She walked out of the kitchen and into the living room where her oldest daughter, her granddaughter, and her son-in-law were watching *Blippi* on the television.

"So what did he say this time?" her daughter asked.

Blippi was telling everyone about kayaking and boat safety, and her granddaughter didn't even look up.

"Same o', same o'," Gabriele said, sitting down with her granddaughter on the wicker sofa.

"You okay, Mom?" her daughter asked, looking concerned.

"Good as I can be. I'm sure I'll survive."

She turned her attention to her granddaughter, who was making paddling motions with her arms. The kids stayed another half hour then left for their home. They knew how sad Gabriele was, something they hadn't seen for many years, but didn't know what they could do. Her daughter cursed Dillard for doing this to her mom and with her next breath wished him well and a speedy return. In truth, the whole family had fallen under Dillard's spell, and his absence was hard on all of them.

Gabriele turned the TV off after they left. She turned the lights out in the kitchen and living room then went back to her bedroom. She was determined not to cry this time. She went into the bathroom and washed up. She finished brushing her teeth and took off her capris and blouse. Clad only in her underwear, she went back into the bedroom, throwing her clothes in a hamper in the open closet. She took off her bra and slipped one of Dillard's T-shirts over her head. The shirt made her feel closer to him, but when she lay down, the warmth from his body was missing.

"Wherever you really are and whatever you are really doing, be safe, my love, and come back to me," she said quietly to the night and turned out the lamp.

Chapter 32

Dillard missed Gabriele. He had an ache in his heart that he had never had before. His job required that he partitioned his emotions; otherwise, they would affect his ability to do what he had to do. Normally, that wasn't a problem, but now her presence was so missed that it threatened to overwhelm his defenses. Forcing himself to think of his current situation, he pushed thoughts of Gabriele aside, knowing that it was up to him to keep everyone safe.

The night passed. He was up and dressed when Rollie knocked on his door. He had told Rollie he didn't have to get him each morning; he was capable of finding his way to the cafeteria in a timely manner. But here he was again. Dillard opened the door and saw that Rollie was dressed in combat gear. He was also armed, and the NATO armband was in place. Dillard headed to the cafeteria with Rollie. Tom was seated, and as usual, the agents were missing. He brewed a cup of coffee and sat down next to Tom. Rollie joined him.

"What did you find in the tunnel, Rollie?" he asked, taking a sip of coffee.

"I went all the way to the train terminal in Vinnytsia. The tunnel comes out about a block from the rail station. The trains are down to one every four hours except for medical trains, which have no set schedule. Soldiers check everyone at the major stops on that line. There are no trains going towards Odessa except medical trains. A switching terminal is in the town, and I saw four engines, several boxcars, and a dozen passenger cars side-railed on parallel tracks at the terminal."

"Thanks, Rollie. Mike, didn't you work for Southern Pacific back in the States?"

"Uhh, yeah, I worked as a conductor for two summers," he said.

"Did you ever do any engineer training?" Dillard asked him.

"A little. We all got to hook up and move a boxcar from a parallel track to the main line and back using the shunters. I probably never went more than a mile."

"Were they diesel-electric engines?" Dillard asked.

"Yeah, that's pretty much all we used at the yard."

"Mike, I need you to do something for me, and I need it done now. I want you and Rollie to go back down the tunnel to town and find out what type of engines are in the yard. Can you do that?"

"I guess. I figure you also want to know how hard it would be to make one run, right?"

"Right," Dillard said.

"What the hell are you thinking, Dillard?" Tom asked.

"Just making backup plans, Tom."

"So what do you think will happen next, Dillard?" Tom asked.

"I think the Russians will back off for now, but that's just temporary. At some point, they will move a large force here, and there will be no stopping it. They'll notify the Israelis and US that they're coming. The US/Israeli presence won't stop them since there is a war going on, and they can make it look like just more attacks on Ukraine. Plus, we've been warned."

Chapter 33

Dillard ate lunch alone. After he finished, he headed back to the security office, and only Tom was there, dressed in combat fatigues and watching the monitors. He turned when Dillard came in.

"You okay, boss?" Tom said, still trying to understand what Dillard had in mind. Dillard ignored the question.

"Anything going on here?" He pointed to the monitors.

"Nothing new," Tom said. "Our guys are building a camp down at the start of the road, and the Russians haven't been back. The Ukrainians sent a colonel up here to check on us, but we didn't let him in. They had heard the explosions yesterday, but I told him all was okay, and he went back to town. Captain Rossof has called a couple of times, wants you to call him soon as you can."

"How about Mike and Rollie? Did they get off?"

"They left about two hours ago. Rollie said they'd probably take about four hours to get there, look around, and get back. Mike seems to think he knows what you want. Anyway, we have no way to reach them until they come back." He picked up the SAT phone and dialed.

"Fill me in on what the hell happened yesterday, Dillard," Rossof said without preamble.

"We had uninvited guests, about fourteen in all. They won't be back, but I expect the next visit will have some real muscle."

"I got word that two armored battalions are mobilizing to move from the Donbas region, but we don't know where exactly they'll go."

"Oh, I think we both know where they're heading. Predictions on how much time we have?"

Rossof didn't like the question, but he knew he had to answer. "We figure about four days, Dillard."

"Okay, sir," Dillard said, "we'll be ready."

"What do you mean 'ready'? There is no way you could resist that size of force, and we can't do anything about it without starting World War III."

"I should be able to tell you our plans tonight. I'm waiting for some intelligence before we discuss it."

"I don't like being left in the dark, Dillard," Rossof said angrily.

"Sir, as soon as I know, you will know." He disconnected the line, having nothing more to say.

Mike and Rollie got back just at dark. They found Dillard, and he got Dr. Evans, and they headed for the security room where Tom was.

"I heard from Captain Rossof that the Russians are mobilizing a force from the Donbas region. He said it looks like two armored battalions. The US doesn't know where they will head, but it's a good guess that they're coming our way." Dillard paused. "That gives us about four days to figure out how we're going to survive. We can't fight a force like that, so the only alternative is to flee. We have the tunnel that gets us into the town of Vinnytsia, but that doesn't help. They'll tear the town apart looking for us. We have to leave the area, and there's only one way to do that: steal a train and take it to Odessa."

He waited for the uproar to die down.

"There is no other way. Don't fight me on this. We don't have the time. Mike, I need your ideas on how we will steal the engine. How many people can the engine hold?"

Mike scratched his head. "Well, there's only room for about four at the most."

"So you're saying we have to hook up a car to it?"

"Well, yes, since we have eight people. But why Odessa?"

"Because it's a seaport, and a boat is our only way out of the country," Dillard said.

"But the Russians have a blockade in the Black Sea there," Tom said.

"So I guess we'll just have to be sneaky." He walked over to the terminals.

"Mike, come here a minute, would you," Dillard said.

Mike walked over. Tom and Dr. Evans were still talking about the plan.

"I need to get all eight people on the engine. We won't have time to hook up any cars. I need you to figure it out, and that means another trip to town. I don't need to tell how you how dangerous that is."

"I really don't need to, Dillard," Mike said. "These are older-style engines. They used to configure them for an engineer, fireman, second man, and conductor. Of course, they don't use the second man or conductor, but that is how they were configured. So the cab can seat four people, but if we all stand, we can get eight in there. It just won't be comfortable."

"Perfect," Dillard said. He turned back to Tom, Rollie, and Dr. Evans, who were arguing.

"Here's the deal. Tomorrow morning at 5:00 a.m., six of us, including Yarslova, are going to walk down that tunnel to Vinnytsia. Two will have already gone on to get the train engine ready to go. We're going to board it and leave for Odessa. We will have no time for anything else. Odessa is 370 miles, not far really, and if the Russians don't realize what we're doing, we will be fine. There won't be any food or toilets, and we'll be packed in like sardines, but it could just save our lives, and it's the only option we have. Dr. Evans, you and I need to talk to Mr. Putin and explain what will be happening tomorrow. I won't allow him to jeopardize the rest of us, and if he has to be unconscious to cooperate, I can take care of that."

She looked upset but nodded her understanding.

"Let's get ready, people. No bags, handguns only. Tom, I'll come back and explain what we're doing about the site. Mike, I'll come back and talk to you and Dave about tomorrow. Dr. Evans, let's go see Yarslova."

Chapter 34

Mike and Dillard left the site at 3:30 a.m., international time. They were armed with sidearms only. Walking the 1.2 kilometers in a rock tunnel was unnerving. It was so dark that their headlamps only lit four feet in front of them. And the silence. All they could hear was their footfalls on the gravel. They talked little and thought a lot. Dillard was going to provide security while Mike picked out an engine and did his research. Once the engine was decided on, Mike would work on how to get onto the main track while Dillard figured out how to keep the station tower from seeing what they were up to. It was critical that they remained undiscovered as long as possible. The Ukrainians wouldn't know who was stealing a locomotive and would assume the worst. All the sidetracks had electric brakes that the tower could initiate. If they didn't get to the main line before being discovered, the tower would set the brakes and send soldiers to investigate.

The other problem was knowing the train schedules. They would be on the western line, and any rail traffic would be going in the same direction. Many people were trying to get out of Vinnytsia, but those transports only ran once every four hours. The problem was the medical trains transporting the injured from the front lines to the Odessa medical center. They didn't have a set schedule. If Dillard's crew could get on the track behind one of them, they'd go straight to Odessa without stopping. Those trains didn't pick anyone up.

Mike also had to figure out how to get eight people inside a cab built for four. Temperatures weren't too bad, but riding openly at four degrees Celsius with a wind blowing would freeze anyone after a while. They all had to be inside. He also had to figure out how to start and run an engine he had never seen and was certainly labeled in a foreign language. And what about fuel? Mike was betting that these engines were serviced before being parked in case they had to leave quickly. Dillard didn't know how Mike would figure all this out, but they were all pushing the impossible.

They got to the end of the tunnel at 4:45 a.m. Dillard looked out at the train-loading platform attached to a ticket office and gift shop. Nobody was around. They would have to go past the platform and around back to the switching yard. It would be fenced and have a locked gate. Dillard figured he could jimmy the lock, but they would have to remain unseen when they crossed Batozka Street, one of the main streets in this part of town. The problem was that Vinnytsia had a population of over 370,000 thousand people, so it was likely someone would be active.

Mike and Dillard had removed the NATO armbands; they were wearing nondescript coveralls that wouldn't stand out. Just a couple of city workers, hopefully. Their sidearms were concealed inside their jumpers.

They made it to the fenced train yard unseen. Dillard could see the control tower for the train yard, and he knew it would be manned. He would have to come up with a distraction. He left Mike after unlocking the gate and went toward the tower. He went around the building to the back side that faced away from the switching yard. He couldn't see Mike, so he had to figure out how to know when they were ready for the distraction. He figured they had about an hour and a half before workers started showing up. Fortunately, because of the war, no one was in a hurry to get to work because the terminal was probably on Russia's hit list. That worked in Dillard's favor.

He crouched down behind a parked car that blocked him from the tower. He'd rig the car up so the gas tank would explode. First he had to see if there was any gas in the tank. Taking out a nail he had in his pocket, he crawled under the back of the car and found the gas line. He twisted the point of the nail against the rubber gas line until it started to drip.

Good, there's probably enough fuel in the tank to cause a good fire. He'd rig up a fuse for the gas filler and one for the dripping gas underneath. But he needed to be sure it would be noticed. To be safe, he took an old shirt out of the unlocked car and crawled back under the car. A small puddle had formed under the hose he had punctured. He used the rag to soak up as much as he could, then crawled back out, and stood up. He opened the passenger door and stuffed the gas-soaked rag in the crack between the top and bottom of the vinyl seat. He used the hand crank and lowered the window halfway down then closed the door. Dillard opened the gas-filler door and saw that there was no locking gas cap. Now he just needed fuses.

Chapter 35

Mike looked at the locomotives parked on the secondary rails. The one in front was an old Russian M62 diesel-electric engine. Mike knew a little about them because they had been exported to many countries back in the '90s. Primarily a freight hauler, it could be used in single- or multiple-engine configurations. His only issue was speed. It was only rated at about sixty miles per hour, and they would be in a hurry. The next two engines were both 40 GE TE33AC diesel-electric locomotives from Wabtec. They were newer engines, probably only a few years old. While not speed demons, he knew they were supposed to go about seventy-five, probably the best he could do with freight haulers. Also, they would be labeled in Ukrainian, but the controls would be similar to freight haulers he had trained on in the US.

He went over to the second engine. The switcher for the secondary track to the main line track was manual, so he'd be able to pull it out on the main line fairly easily. But as soon as he switched the tracks, an alarm would go off in the control tower, alerting them. He hoped Dillard's distraction would be enough to occupy their attention for a few minutes while they made their escape.

Mike carefully climbed up into the cab of the second train, being careful to stay out of sight of the tower. Inside the layout was what he had expected. Looking around, he figured they could get eight people inside standing. It would be tight but doable. He switched on the auxiliary power, and the fuel gauges registered full. That was what he had hoped because these were hungry beasts. He looked over the notched throttle system. It would automatically engage the transmission once he moved the throttle out of the idle position. Okay, no big surprises. He threw out some of the gear they didn't need for more room. Hopefully, no one would get to work early and see the pile beside the locomotive.

Dillard took another bullet out of the cartridge and poured the gunpowder on the old paper plate. He had a small pile of powder from the nine cartridges, hopefully enough for his fuses. He wanted to make two, one for the gas-soaked rag in the front seat and one for the gas tank. He had stuffed dry paper in the neck of the gas tank filler, leaving a hole for the homemade fuse to plug into.

The fuse was several plastic straws stuck together, which he would fill with gunpowder. His only concern was that the plastic straw might melt before the gunpowder could burn up and ignite the gas. He cut a short piece of straw and filled it with the powder. He put it on the sidewalk and lit one end. The powder immediately flared and started burning. It burned faster than the plastic melted, so Dillard thought it would probably work. By putting three straws together, he had a tube about two and a half feet long. That was for the gas tank. The other fuse was about eighteen inches because he wanted the upholstery to start burning first.

Dillard looked at his watch. He had about forty minutes until everyone was to be at the engine. He hoped that end went okay. He decided to sneak over and check on Mike. He put the fuses under the car. It was still dark with no moon, so he didn't think they would be seen. He needed to let Mike know what he was up to.

Dr. Evans was third in line in the tunnel. She had a little trouble with Yarslova, but the urgency of the issue sank in finally. He didn't give her any more trouble. The rest of the team and security guys knew that if they stayed at the site, they would most likely die.

Rollie was in the lead, Dave at the rear. She couldn't see Rollie in the dark tunnel, but she knew he was up there in front somewhere. She almost ran into Myrna, who had stopped in front of her.

"We're here, Lee," she whispered. She could hear soft murmurs from in front somewhere. Suddenly, Rollie appeared in her light.

"We are to wait here for Mike or Dillard to take us to the train," he said.

She nodded her understanding. They all just huddled together in the cold, dark tunnel, waiting for what they hoped would be a train ride to Odessa.

Chapter 36

Dillard filled Mike in on the plan to burn the car. He thought the fuse would give him about eight minutes to get back here. Mike told Dillard that it was his job to switch the rails when he gave him the signal then jump onto the moving engine. They planned to go to a side spur far enough from Vinnytsia and wait for a medical train then pull in behind it. Mike briefed; Dillard headed back to the parked car.

Mike sneaked back to the passenger loading platform. Still no one was around, so he went around the back and over to the tunnel entrance. He hadn't noticed the signs telling everyone to stay away all around the entrance. Rollie saw him coming and let the group know to get ready. Mike told them some of the plan and said to follow him to the engine. They had to be careful not to be seen. They'd cross the road two at a time.

The walk to the switching yard went as planned. They all took care not to be seen by people in the terminal building and made it to the TE33AC without incident. They crossed in front and went up into the cab.

"Wow, if we weren't friends before, we sure will be after this ride," Frank said, wedging himself between Myrna and Dr. Evans.

Mike checked his watch. Dillard was supposed to light the fuse in about five minutes, then run for the track switcher, and throw the lever. Mike turned on the ignition, let the glow plugs get hot, and hit the starter. All sixteen cylinders came to life with a loud roar. It was 6:15 a.m.

Dillard checked his watch. It was time. He opened the door and lit the fuse for the gas rag in the upholstery. It started sputtering. He closed the door and turned to the straw stuck in the gas tank. He lit the end, and it, too, started sputtering and burning up toward the tank. Time to go.

He raced behind the tower building and through the gate into the switching yard. He could hear the TE33AC rumbling but didn't think the tower would notice. He went over to the switching box and waited for

Mike's signal. It was getting lighter, and he thought the car should do its thing soon. No sooner had he thought this than a loud bang went off and he could see light from the flames around the side of the building.

Mike heard it also and selected the first position on the throttle. The engine began to move. Dillard saw him move and threw the handle of the track switcher to the down position. Nothing happened. He quickly looked at the switching mechanism and saw where a key was supposed to be inserted to make the lever engage. He had no key, but he still had his penknife. Meanwhile, the engine was getting closer. If Dillard couldn't get the track to switch, they were done.

He opened the penknife but selected the little screwdriver, not the blade. He pulled the switching lever back to its original position and shoved the screwdriver blade into the keyhole. He tried to lower the lever back down, but it resisted. Using all his strength, he managed to get the lever to lower and heard the screech of the rails moving. When he turned toward the engine, it was only ten feet away. The train was moving slowly, and he had no trouble jumping onto the side brace and climbing over the electrical box to the door to the cab. He was able to get most of his body inside as Mike started moving the throttle notch by notch. They were on the main track.

Mike got the engine up to sixty-five, about as fast as he would go. They were using over 150 gallons per hour, but they had sufficient fuel to carry them to Odessa. Yarslova seemed to be enjoying the ride. Dillard guessed that he'd never had to flee for his life before, and it seemed he was taking it all in as an adventure. Problem is, if they weren't successful, the adventure would come to an end in a very unpleasant way. He had no doubt that the Russians would prefer Yarslova dead rather than in US hands. He doubted that young Mr. Putin had thought about that.

The countryside whizzed by. Part of Dillard's body was hot; the other half was cold, but that was the least of his worries. He was amazed that their quickly hashed out plan had worked so far. Now they had to find a spur and pull off the main line and wait for a medical train. He reminded Mike to watch for a siding.

They had traveled about sixteen miles when Mike spotted a sign for a siding. He couldn't read what it said, but the picture of a train pulling off told him all he needed. The engine started to slow down. They were doing thirty miles per hour when they got to the siding entrance. If they had been hauling freight, they never would have made it into the siding at that speed. Mike pulled the train in and stopped about two hundred feet inside the pullout. He moved the throttle down to idle and told the group they could get off for a few minutes but be ready to go quickly. Everyone except Yarslova, Mike, and Dillard got down.

"Mr. Ross," Yarslova said, turning to him suddenly, "don't think that I do not know the stakes of this escape. I know my father, and he will not hesitate to kill all of us in order to keep his secrets."

Dillard smiled at him. "I wondered if you did, Yarslova. You seemed to be enjoying this adventure a little too much."

"Enjoying? No, Mr. Ross, but I do appreciate the situation we are in, and I find humor in it."

"What humor is there about running for your life, Yarslova?" Dillard asked.

"The humor is that the man I have read much about but is no longer considered a threat by my father and others is the very man who is doing the impossible and stealing me away. Don't you see the irony of it?" He laughed.

Chapter 37

Everyone had gotten out of the engine cab for a few minutes. Dillard told them to come back into the cab, but he and Rollie would wait outside to give the others more room. The train was idling, and Mike was ready to give chase to the medical train when it came by. Rollie and Dillard spoke quietly outside, getting to know each other. Rollie was from Des Moines and had been in the Army for six years. He was a sergeant first class. He said Mike was also a sergeant first class. Dave was a lance corporal, and Tom was a sergeant major. The four of them had been assigned to a support group stationed in Kiev a month ago; new orders put them at the archaeological site in Vinnytsia. All they were told was that US intelligence was running an interrogation on a defector and they were there to provide security. They weren't told who the defector was, only that he was a high-value asset. No one was supposed to know about the operation, so the security detail should have been routine. But all that had changed. Now they were fleeing through war-torn Ukraine on a stolen train with the Russian president's son and hundreds of Russian soldiers trying to stop them.

Dillard felt rather than heard the medical train coming. He climbed off the train and put his cheek on the rail. He could feel the vibration from their engine, but he could tell there was a second vibration, which seemed to be getting stronger. He stood up and climbed back up to the engine.

"Company coming, Mike," he said.

Tom started moving people around in the cab to make room for Dillard and Rollie. Mike was watching the mirrors. He didn't know how many cars would be attached to the engine, so he would just watch for the last one then inch the throttle forward after it passed. They couldn't accelerate until they were on the main tracks.

Everyone was tense.

What if it isn't the medical train? Tom thought. *It could be the Russians or the Ukraine soldiers on a military train trying to overtake us. Guess we'd better hope for the best.*

Mike could see flashes of light reflected on the train's metal. It was still too far away to tell what type of train it was. They'd know soon enough. Dillard checked his .45, Rollie and Tom following suit.

The oncoming train was about a quarter mile away. Mike could make out a little detail, and he could see a red cross painted on the nose of the engine.

"Looks like the medical train, Dillard," Mike said.

Everyone relaxed a little except Dillard, who never seemed nervous.

"Okay, people, hang on to something. It's going to get bumpy," Mike told them, preparing to chase the last car of the train.

He counted fourteen cars and, as the last one passed, started accelerating slowly. Then the rear wheels touched the main tracks. Mike moved the throttle all the way up to full power. The train jerked as it tried to compensate for the surge of power. He kept one hand on the brake handle and the other on the throttle as the train sped up. It was no race car, but the train hit sixty in a short time with no freight cars attached. Mike had estimated the medical train's speed somewhere around fifty miles per hour. They still had over two hundred miles to Odessa, so plenty of time to catch the other train. They hoped to use it as cover.

Forty-four miles later, Dillard saw the last car of the medical train about half a mile ahead. He told Mike to keep that distance between them. If it stopped for some reason, they needed enough time to stop their engine. Also, he didn't want someone on that train getting curious about a locomotive following them.

Rollie wormed his way back to Dillard.

"So what happens when we reach Odessa, Dillard?"

"We'll ditch the engine before the train station and go into town. We need to find a place to hold up while some of us explore the port for transportation. When we find a boat, we'll try to reach Varna, Bulgaria, in Eastern Europe. Bulgaria would not be my first choice normally because of their political history, but beggars can't be choosers. If Captain Rossof can arrange local support there, we'll be okay. At least we'll be out of Ukraine, and it won't be easy for Russia to pin us down there. First I'm going to call Captain Rossof to find out how hot the Odessa port is." Dillard got out the SAT phone and dialed.

"Go, Dillard," Rossof said, not wasting words.

"We are approximately two hundred miles from Odessa. We are traveling in a Ukrainian locomotive stolen from the Vinnytsia train yard and are following one of the medical trains that take the wounded to the hospital facility in Odessa. By now the Ukrainians would know the engine is missing but not where it is going. It's the Russians that worry me. I expect they will get to the archaeological site within two days, and then they'll start canvassing all the nearby towns. The missing train is bound to be reported, so we'd better be off of it. They'll use aircraft to find the train, which won't take them long unless the Ukrainians shoot them down. We can always hope."

"Condition of the asset?"

"Safe and secure as the rest of us."

"Needs, Chief?"

"Friendly local asset to provide a boat. We want to make for Varna, Bulgaria, in Eastern Europe, but I don't know the conditions in Odessa or, for that matter, Bulgaria."

"Conditions are not good, Chief. Two days ago, a Russian ship destroyed the small Ukrainian military base on Snake Island. They have a blockade set up in the Black Sea, and nothing is getting in or out of the ports."

"Not surprised, sir. The ports are critical to Russia if they want to invade from the south."

"I can probably get you a boat locally, but there isn't much the US can do as far as getting you through the blockade. If you can make it to Varna, we have assets there that can keep you safe. Russia is on friendly terms with Bulgaria, and there is a large Russian population in Varna, so you'll have to go dark."

"Understood, Captain, the local help is appreciated. I'll check in later." Dillard cut the line.

Chapter 38

They had followed the medical train for 190 miles through the Ukraine countryside. Most of the time, there wasn't much to see except melting snow on bare fields. The few towns they passed were still bottled up because of the weather and the Russians. Winter still had a grip on the countryside, but it was starting to loosen, and the roads and trails they passed were muddy with puddles of melting snow and ice.

Dillard told Mike to start watching the train ahead more carefully. It might start slowing down, and they didn't want to get caught unawares. He contacted Rossof again and was briefed on where to meet the local asset.

Dillard took inventory of the people crowded in the train cab. Everyone was dressed for the weather with warm coats, gloves, and waterproof boots. At least he wouldn't have to worry about that. They had no baggage except for the backpack that he had Dave bring.

"Listen up, folks," Dillard said loudly, trying to compete with the noisy engine. "We'll be near Odessa soon, and once we stop, we have to make our way to the town of Deribasovka without being noticed. We should be able to stop the engine fairly close to the town, even though it will tip off the Russians as to our location once they start looking for us. We are still under the Russian radar, but that will be changing soon.

"The US has arranged for us to meet a local asset there named Sergi Lopov, and he will supply shelter until later tonight. He is going to get us to a boat near the Khadjibey estuary, which we will use to get to Bulgaria. The trip through Odessa Bay will be in the dark, and he's providing intel on the location of the Russian blockade ships, which we have to avoid. Our direction is away from the ships, and the boat is small enough that their radars shouldn't classify us as a threat. The trip to Varna will take us about twenty-eight hours, and once we are past the blockade, we can travel faster.

However, if our escape from Vinnytsia is discovered by the Russians, they will be on high alert and either sink or board us. Rossof tells me that the Russian troops are still a day away from Vinnytsia, so if luck is with us, we'll be out of the bay before they find out."

"But even if we get past the blockade, won't the Russian Air Force come looking for us?" Tom asked.

"Probably, but we'll stay as close to the coastline as we can."

None of the people in the cab looked confident about the plan. Dillard turned his attention back to the train in front of him.

Mike suddenly said, "Dillard, the train ahead is starting to slow down. The next town should be Deribasovka."

"Okay, folks, let's get ready to get off the train. The town will be on our left, and there is only one wire fence we have to cross to get to the road. Yarslova, you stay behind with me. Tom, you lead the group to the road. Yarslova and I will catch up with you on the road. Sergi will be driving a Toyota minivan, light blue. Find him and get in the van as quickly as you can." He and Yarslova wormed their way to the back of the group.

Mike was slowing the engine down. They could see the outline of a small town ahead on their left. The medical train was out of sight. He pulled the throttle back a notch at a time, dropping about fifteen miles per hour each time. He was rolling up to the east end of the town when he put it in notch one and applied the brake lever slowly, more to keep the noise of the brakes down than to make a smooth stop. The engine came to a halt, and he set the parking brake and killed the ignition. They could hear the sound of the metal contraction as it began cooling.

Tom was out of the cab and on the slushy ground within seconds. Dr. Evans and the rest of the group came behind, with Mike bringing up the rear. Dillard and Yarslova waited in the cab until the group crossed in front of the engine and headed for the four-foot wire fence. Tom had it down in less than a minute, and the rest of the group climbed over the bent wire. Dillard motioned for Yarslova to go first, and they exited the cab and started for the downed fence. They could see the group up on the road running toward an abandoned barn, looking for cover. Dillard and Yarslova came behind them, and luckily, there was no one in sight.

When they got to the building, the rest of the group was inside the partially collapsed barn, screened from the road. Tom was at the corner, looking down the road. He waved to Dillard, indicating that he saw their ride. Dillard told them that they'd draw less attention if they just walked up to the van normally and got inside. Tom stepped out, followed by Dr.

Evans and the rest of the group. Again, Dillard and Yarslova brought up the rear.

Ten feet from the van, a man got out and came around, opening the side door. They could see that there were no seats, giving them enough room to get inside. Dillard had Yarslova get into the front passenger seat.

Sergi turned to them, smiling, and said, "Welcome to Deribasovka, my friends," in broken English and quickly turned back, got in the driver's seat, and they started moving.

Sergi took them through town and turned up a muddy road that led them to a small farm about a quarter mile from Deribasovka. Inside they found Sergi's wife preparing a hot meal. She smiled at them but didn't speak English, so Dillard spoke to her in Russian.

"Anna says there are clean towels in the washroom and there's plenty of hot water. I suggest everyone try to get a shower because you won't get another chance for quite some time." He spoke to Anna again. "Lunch will be about twenty minutes."

Everyone, including Dillard, took turns with the shower. When they were finished, Anna had prepared borscht with deruni (or potato pancakes) and sour cream and holubtsi stuffed with lamb. The smell of the lamb and cabbage made Dillard drool. She had made enough for at least a dozen people.

Yarslova was the first to grab a plate and bowl and start filling them. Dillard waited patiently then filled his plate with deruni and holubtsi. Never having developed a taste for borscht, a soup made from beetroot, he passed it up but noticed everyone else filled their bowls. They ate and talked of home and family. Anna, Sergi, and Yarslova talked about Ukraine and the Russian invasion. Dillard thought it was interesting that Yarslova went to great pains to hide his true identity from them and spoke sympathetically about the war.

After lunch, Dillard told everyone to try to nap. They'd start for the boat at 7:00 p.m., not late enough to arouse suspicion but dark enough to hide their movements. Sergi said Odessa was like a ghost town because of the blockade and fear of attack by the Russians. Most Ukrainians were home with locked doors by 7:00 p.m.

The group disbursed and found places to lie down. Sergi and Dillard went back into the kitchen. Anna fixed them coffee, and they started discussing the plan for the evening. Sergi made no secret that he thought their chances of making Varna were slim, but he didn't question their reasons. Several of the local fishermen had agreed to take their boats out of the estuary at the same time Dillard left to further hide their escape. Those boats would go in opposite directions to different parts of the coast. All the boats were relatively the same size. Sergi also had the maritime maps and wave and storm predictions, something Dillard was hoping for. Storms in Odessa Bay and the Black Sea could turn murderous this time of year, but it looked like they had a thirty-hour window before the next heavy squalls were expected.

Dillard went into the hallway near the back room and lay down on the floor. He was conditioned to rest when and where he could, and he was at once asleep. In what seemed like just a few minutes, Tom woke him.

"We're packed and ready to go, Dillard."

The group was in the small living room talking to Sergi and Anna. They said their thanks and goodbyes and went out to the van. It was dark but still relatively early. Sergi got in the driver's seat, with Rollie next to him. They all had their dirty winter clothes on, and it was pretty stuffy in the van even after the showers. He pulled away from the house and drove back down the road toward town, but when they got to the intersection, they turned left toward Odessa.

The estuary was about six miles from Sergi's house. They drove about forty-five miles per hour, a safe speed on the slushy roads. Several cars and one pickup passed them from the opposite direction, but no one was behind or in front of them going toward Odessa. It wasn't safe to be out on the streets in town after dark. They passed several turnoffs to Odessa's city center and kept driving toward the ports.

They had passed several signs for estuaries, and Sergi began to slow down and turned right off the main road toward Khadjibey estuary. The van went about a mile, and the road came to an end near the rock outcroppings that made up the estuary walls. The rocks helped block the winds and surf off the bay, protecting the fishing boats that were tied up there. Dillard could see five boats tied up to the rocks.

Sergi pointed to the second one in line and said, "твой." ("Yours.")

Dillard got out first and looked around. It was hard to make anything out in the dark except the white of the surf breaking on the sandy beach and rocks. He saw no other people, but there were dim lights on several of the boats, including the one waiting for them. Everybody got out of the van except Sergi and Rollie. Dillard walked around to his side of the van and shook Sergi's hand through the open window. He turned and went back to the passenger side. Rollie had his window down.

"Are you sure of this, Rollie?" Dillard asked for the fifth time.

Rollie had decided to stay in Deribasovka with Sergi and his wife. He would make his way back to Vinnytsia in a few weeks. Dillard said he'd let the base know. They shook hands, and he started walking out on the rock estuary. It was wet and slippery, and the men helped the women over the rocks to the boat. Dillard saw a silhouette in the first boat when he passed by. He climbed down onto the deck and turned to help the others climb off the rocks and onto the boat. Everyone made it, so he turned back and opened the door to the pilothouse.

Their boat had candle lanterns lit inside the pilothouse, which was about ten feet long and eight feet wide. Like most of the fishing boats here, the roof of the pilothouse was only about six feet high to offer less surface to the constant winds.

Bending down slightly, he went inside and over to the captain's chair. The rest of the group came inside and sat on the makeshift seats. They were produce crates set under the windows on each side of the cabin.

The front windscreen was hinged and could be opened for fresh air when the weather was warm. Dillard looked at the controls. They were simple: just a throttle, a shift lever, and indicators for fuel and engine temperature. There was a toggle switch for the single windshield wiper with an electric motor and a toggle switch for the running lights. A cheap compass sat in a plastic holder mounted above the steering wheel. There was no radio.

Dillard turned the ignition key on, checking the fuel. As he expected, it was full. Sergi said the boat was outfitted with two oversize tanks, which would give him a range of more than three hundred nautical miles. That should get them to Varna. He knew the small four-cylinder diesel would not be fast, but it was sturdy and reliable, and that was more important than speed. They wouldn't be trying to outrun ships, and they couldn't afford to break down. He turned the ignition back off.

"Dave, I need an inventory of the stores they packed in here."

"Coming up, sir—I mean, Dillard." He began looking at the stacked cardboard boxes up near the bow.

Dillard took out the chart Sergi had given him. The tide was coming in and was due to be full by 8:30 p.m. They had about twenty minutes to prepare.

Chapter 39

Captain Rossof knew the odds of Dillard Ross making it to Varna were slim to none, but Ross had performed miracles before. He didn't know of any other person that would have a better chance. Their hands were tied. The US couldn't operate openly in the Ukrainian territories without the chance of creating an international incident. He was doing everything he could, but ultimately, it would be up to the chief to get them through.

Using a nonmilitary person to do this was the DOD's idea. Sure, Dillard had a military background, but he was way past the expected age of action, or so they would assume. They would be very wrong, of course, but it still helped with deniability should they fall into Russian hands. Dr. Evans was a different problem. She had information that was sensitive to US intelligence and could not be permitted to be captured. Chief Ross knew the score there. It was his job to make sure she didn't, one way or another. But would he?

They said you shouldn't look a gift horse in the mouth, but this gift had a lot of strings attached. He didn't envy Chief Ross. Rossof smiled. Dillard always got mad when he called him Chief, but that was the Dillard Ross he remembered, and he would always be Chief Warrant Officer Dillard Ross to him.

Chapter 40

Their Ukrainian friends had packed enough food for at least four days, four gallons of fresh water, some light fishing tackle, blankets, and an old Coleman lantern with a can of white gas and replacement elements. They also left them an old AK assault rifle and four clips of ammunition. Dillard could just picture them squaring off with a Russian missile cruiser with the AK, but you never know.

He had checked the chart that Sergi marked up. They would have to stay about thirty yards off the shore for enough depth. He was hoping that their small size and direction and the clutter created by the coastline would let them evade Russian interest. There was only one way to find out.

He turned the ignition on, letting the glow plugs warm up then hit the starter. The engine caught immediately and idled smoothly. Overspray had coated the windshield with salty brine, and he flipped the toggle, and it scrapped the accumulation off enough to see out. But there was nothing to see. He could see the estuary outline because of the waves breaking on the rocks. He'd turn the boat west once they were past the end of the estuary and try to stay parallel to the shoreline. He asked Tom and Mike to clean the windows to help him navigate. Dave went out of the cabin and untied the bow and stern lines. When he signaled to Dillard that they were loose, he put the boat in gear and fed it a little fuel. Turning the bow away from the estuary, he headed away from shore slowly. Dave came back inside and told him the other boats were coming out behind them. Everyone had their running lights off.

They plowed slowly through the cold, inky water. There was enough wind to form small whitecaps, but the swells were only a few feet tall, and the old boat plowed through them with ease. Inside the pilothouse, it was warm, mostly because of the eight warm bodies crammed into it. Whenever Dillard went out on deck, he was quickly reminded of the biting wind and cold sea spray. Still, it had been a good trip so far, but he guessed they had only gone about seven miles from their launch site.

Back out on deck, he tried to use the overhang of the pilothouse to screen some of the spray so he could use the night vision scope. He scanned the horizon, which he knew was directly north of him. His orientation came from the waves breaking on the shore and rocks, and even in total darkness, he could make out the faint line of surf.

He searched from east to west. At about thirty degrees to the shoreline, he could see a faint outline of a ship. If it wasn't silhouetted against the horizon, he wouldn't have seen it. It was big but didn't seem to be moving.

Probably the Moskva missile cruiser, he thought.

He calculated that it was three miles from them. The cruiser's searchlights wouldn't reach their boat, but the radar probably had them painted. He just hoped that his assumption about their size and direction would be enough to let them slide by. He had no doubt that the Moskva would take them out with the first launch should they decide this small boat was a threat. Rossof had told him that Presidents Putin and Zelenskyy were planning talks, so maybe that would make them less trigger-happy.

The Russian troops wouldn't get to Vinnytsia until this afternoon. When they did, there would be nowhere to hide anywhere near Odessa on land or sea. Dillard went back inside and told the team about the ship and his hunch that they'd be let through. Everyone hoped he was right.

At 2:00 a.m., Mike took Dillard's place at the helm. They had used about one-fourth of their fuel, the engine temp was fine, and they were making a solid ten knots through relatively smooth seas. Dillard went back on deck and again scanned the horizon. He couldn't see any outlines of ships, but he knew they could still see him on their radar. It was amazing that Ukrainian fishermen still fished at night in this weather. If that hadn't been the case, they would surely have triggered someone's attention. He went back inside. Lee Evans and most of her team were sleeping fitfully, the rocking of the boat helping. They just had to be careful not to fall off the produce crates, but it looked like they had wedged their crates and bodies against each other. Good for them.

Dillard sat down on the floor. He relaxed and let his mind go unguarded, thinking back to Florida and his short time with Gabriele. It was such a different world, one that he didn't really know, but that small taste he sampled was enough to make him want more, much more.

Dillard woke up about two hours later. Nothing had changed in the cabin, but something had brought him out of his sleep on high alert. He sat there a minute, trying to pin down the disturbance. It was the motion of the swells. They had changed and were coming from a different direction. He got to his feet and turned to go out on deck. A small wobble made him stumble.

Something's wrong, he thought. He turned back and saw that Mike had fallen asleep. *Crap*, he thought, quickly moving to the steering helm.

He grabbed Mike's shoulder and shook him, but he didn't wake up. Dillard looked out through the windscreen and saw the outline of the surf on the rocks about thirty feet away. He quickly spun the wheel, heading back out to sea.

They were safely back out a quarter of a mile from land. Mike was still unconscious, and Dillard saw the half-empty water bottle in the cupholder. He picked it up, smelling the water. There was no odor. He poured some on his fingers and tasted it. It was slightly salty. He knew what it was.

GHB (gamma hydroxybutyrate) was a popular date-rape drug back in the '90s. It is a central nervous system depressant that makes you sleepy and slows down breathing and heart rate. In large quantities, it can kill.

Dillard looked at the rest of the team. All of them had been drinking the bottled water put on board by the Ukrainians. He hadn't drunk any because he was out on deck when they got it out of the box. His unopened bottle was lying on a shelf by the door, held down with a bungee cord. No wonder the others were asleep.

He lowered Mike down to the floor and took over driving the boat. They had lost about a mile, but that wasn't a big deal. He wondered what other surprises had been packed on the boat.

Chapter 41

The team was starting to come around. Dillard had just left them where they were. Yarslova was the first to speak.

"I must have been so tired," he said, stretching. Then he looked around and noticed everyone was either sleeping or just waking up.

"How could we all just be waking up?"

"The water was drugged, Yarslova," Dillard replied.

"Drugged? But who would do that and why?" He looked around, a little confused.

"Someone wanted us to run up onto the shore. I wouldn't be surprised if a welcome party was up in the woods someplace," Dillard said. "Do me a favor, I need you to start waking everyone up. There might be other surprises they left for us, and we need to look for them."

They had taken almost everything apart and found nothing. Mike pulled a small box from a shelf in the back.

"This is about it, Dillard," he said, taking off the lid. Inside was a flashlight and spare batteries. "All I see here is a flashlight, and it doesn't even work." He tried to click it on several times.

"Let me see it, Mike," Dillard said, turning to face him. Mike walked over and handed him the flashlight.

"Give me the batteries also," he said.

Mike handed him the box with the batteries. Dillard unscrewed the lens from the light, looking at the bulb. Then he unscrewed the back end of the flashlight. Two C batteries fell out. He picked them up and looked at them. They looked fine. He put the flashlight down and picked up the spare batteries. He noticed the weight difference between the two batteries at once. Looking closely, he could see the heavy battery had a faint line around one end. He grabbed it and twisted it, and it began to unscrew. Inside was a small circuit board with several electronic components. Small wires were connected to it and ran up into the body of the battery. Dillard knew what it was immediately: a position transmitter set for some frequency that was monitored by the people who put it there. He left it connected.

Outside the sky was starting to lighten. The weather report had been right; so far no squalls had threatened them. There was still a constant wind, but they were running with it, so it was a good, not bad, thing. He pulled out the marked-up map that Sergi had given him. It showed landmarks on shore that they could use to orient themselves. In about thirty minutes, it would be bright enough to see. His nightscope didn't work well in half-light.

Tom was organizing breakfast for everyone. They were sticking to the food they had brought from Sergi's house instead of eating the rations left for them on board. This reduced their choices to oatmeal or oatmeal. They had no coffee, but they did have half a dozen tea bags, which would have to do. The oatmeal was in small packets, and they just added hot water to the packet and ate it like that. Dillard hated oatmeal, but he knew he needed the calories, so he ate it anyway. The tea was good and hot thanks to the single propane burner in the boat's galley. He hoped that by tonight, they would be out of dangerous waters.

In a few hours, Dillard expected the Russians to start flying up and down the Ukrainian coast looking for them. He hoped the US-supplied antiaircraft systems would keep them busy. He was still a little surprised that the Moskva hadn't sent helicopters to check them out when they were still in Odessa Bay. Something else must have gotten their attention.

Dillard went out on deck to try to spot a landmark. He had a rough idea of where they were by plotting their course and speed. He figured they were about fifty miles from Mangalia, Romania. That was good and bad news. The bad news was that the Russians would be able to fly in the area without worrying about Ukrainian antiaircraft missiles. The good news was, they were off the coast of Romania. They had another full day of sailing before they got to Varna.

"So you understand what I need, Tom?"

He nodded his head yes and went into the pilothouse. Dillard looked out at the shoreline, the outline of which could now be seen clearly. He turned and went inside.

Mike throttled down the engine and put it in neutral. They wouldn't take the chance of turning it off, but Dillard needed their speed to be slow or nothing. Tom showed him what he had rigged up. It was an old fishing pole and reel with braided line, a half-ounce lead sinker, and a number 1 hook. They didn't have any bait, so he used some of the canned meat the Ukrainians had left. Nobody was going to eat it anyway, not after the doctored water.

He and Tom went out on deck. It was considerably warmer now, near fifty-five degrees, and the wind had lost its bite. Tom went aft and threw the line in. They didn't care what they caught; Dillard just needed a fish to fit his plan. They bobbed around for twenty minutes when the old reel started singing. Tom set the drag and started hauling in the fish. It took a while. There was no net or hook to boat the fish, so he would have to land it the hard way. The fish gave him a fight, and despite the circumstances, Tom was enjoying it. The fish broke out of the water about fifty feet behind the boat. Dillard didn't know what kind of fish it was, but Tom thought it was some sort of mackerel, common in the Black Sea. He got it up to the side of the boat, the fish finally tiring. With one big heave, he got the fish onto the deck.

Dillard rushed over to the fish, trying to hold it down. It was about twenty-four inches long with beautiful silver scales and a black stripe running from tail to gill. Tom dropped the pole and came to help him.

"Let's get the hook out of him first, Tom," Dillard said.

Tom used his fingers to pry open its mouth, trying not to cut himself on the razor-sharp teeth.

The hook came out easily, and he held the fish by its gills while Dillard shoved the battery case with the transmitter down its throat. With that done, Tom picked the fish up and threw it over the side. Dillard didn't know if this would work, but if it did, it would give the Russians a wild-goose chase.

Chapter 42

Throughout that day, they kept an eye out for aircraft. Several times they heard engines but never saw a plane. Maybe Dillard's fish plan had worked. Cloud cover came in at 4:00 p.m., and that helped even more. They had seen the lights of Mangalia about an hour earlier, so they were on schedule. He figured they'd motor through the night and reach Varna early morning. They'd pretend to be fishermen coming in after night fishing, and if lucky, they'd find some boats to join.

Dillard was down in the pilothouse when Mark came in from the deck.

"Dillard, I think I heard a motor somewhere nearby."

Dillard looked up from the steering console. "Could you see anything?"

"No, but it didn't sound like a plane, more like a boat."

Dillard got up from the pilot's seat. "You take over here. I'm going to take a look outside." He walked past Mike and went out through the cabin door.

Outside the clouds and fog obscured both the land and sea around them. He figured their visibility was about one hundred yards. His nightscope was worthless in the dim light, so he just stared across the starboard side of the boat. Tom was searching the port side. He could hear a dull rumble like a big diesel engine at idle, but he couldn't see anything.

"Tell Mike to kill the engine. We'll take the chance that it won't start again. Also, tell everyone to be extra quiet."

Tom went inside to do his bidding. Dillard kept searching in the direction he thought the sound was coming from. The silence was eerie.

The engine sound seemed to come from several directions, probably bouncing off the fog layer, he thought.

He looked over the side of the boat. The waves were calm, just small rollers. He watched the waves for a minute, mesmerized by their movement, but he snapped out of it when he saw a cigarette butt float by.

Oh no, he thought. *We must almost be on top of the other boat.*

He quickly went into the cabin. Fourteen pairs of concerned eyes stared back at him, but no one said anything. He motioned for Tom to follow him back out. Tom was careful to close the door softly.

On deck, Dillard whispered to Tom to get one of the long paddles tied to the railing. Dillard got the other down. He quietly told him that they needed to paddle the boat in the direction of the swells. Tom didn't know why but did as he asked. The boat was too big to make much headway, but the wave action helped them. Dillard wanted to move away from where he thought the cigarette butt had floated from. They both paddled as quietly as they could.

Suddenly, the quiet diesel motor roared to life. Dillard knew they'd been spotted. He knew they couldn't outrun or outfight a Russian trawler, and that's what he thought he heard. Seconds later, they could hear the slap of waves on a hull as the boat approached them.

"Tom, go inside quickly and tell the crew not to resist when we are boarded."

Tom quickly dropped the paddle and went through the cabin door, not bothering to be quiet any longer. Two searchlights suddenly lit up the deck, and Dillard was clearly outlined. He raised his hands. A loudspeaker spoke Russian, telling him to approach the railing and catch the rope that was being thrown to him. He did as instructed. The trawler was close enough now that he could see the soldiers lined up on the sixty-foot deck pointing their assault rifles at him. He counted seven soldiers. When the trawler was twenty feet away, it shut down its engines and a rope was thrown to Dillard. He tied it to one of the turnbuckles on the bow. Another rope was thrown, and he was told to tie it to the rear. The boats were still twenty feet away, but they were locked together by the ropes.

The speaker told him to catch another rope and tie it midship. He did, and as soon as it was tied off, several Russian soldiers started pulling the two boats together. There was a slight bump as the two boats came together against the trawler's rubber fenders. The gap was only one or two feet, depending on the swells. Quickly several armed soldiers jumped the gap and climbed the rail. The other Russians never took their guns off Dillard.

He was quickly bound and made to sit on the deck. Two more armed soldiers came across from the trawler, and they positioned themselves to rush the pilothouse. One of the soldiers called out to the group in the cabin to lay down their arms or they would all be killed. Then he carefully turned the door handle and kicked the door open. Inside seven people stood with their hands up. In minutes, all the passengers were on deck of the fishing boat with rifles pointed at them. Another soldier from the trawler, this one apparently senior, came across. He didn't have an assault rifle, but he had his handgun out. When he got on deck of the fishing boat, he came over to the captives, looking at each one carefully. When he saw Yarslova, he motioned him out of line and made him jump to the other ship. He turned and followed.

All of Dillard's team had been bound and made to sit on the deck next to him. Soldiers had searched the pilothouse, and satisfied, all went back to the trawler except for two who kept their rifles pointed at the bound captives. A few minutes later, another soldier came across from the trawler and took pictures of Dillard and his group with a cell phone then went back to the trawler. They stayed this way for almost an hour, their guards smoking and talking to each other. Dr. Evans had tried to talk to Dillard, but he motioned for her to be quiet.

Dillard knew that one of two things would probably happen now. They would be shot and the fishing boat sunk, or the Russians would take them back to their base for interrogation. If they found out who Dr. Evans was, he knew they would take her back for sure. The rest of them might not be of value and discarded.

Apparently, they hadn't identified Dr. Evans yet, because when the officer came back, he told the soldiers to move all of them into the cabin. It seemed that they were going to tow the fishing boat and its passengers back to a port. They went inside still bound and sat as best they could on the boxes or the floor. The soldiers went back on deck, closing the door. Dillard knew they would post guards to watch the prisoners.

They could feel their boat being moved. It bumped into the trawler several times. Finally, it seemed they had it positioned like they wanted it, and Dillard could feel the forward movement. They must have lashed the rudder so they could tow it behind them. He looked out the window and could tell they were only doing about five knots, so if the Russians planned to take them back to Ukraine, it would be a long haul. The Russians weren't too worried about them escaping; where would they go? There was only one door to the pilothouse, and that was heavily guarded.

Chapter 43

Tom, Dave, and Dillard huddled together talking quietly. Everyone was racking their brains to come up with an escape plan, but it looked pretty hopeless. The group was coming to the conclusion that they would be interrogated and then imprisoned in Russia—that was, all but Dillard Ross. He was too busy figuring out an escape plan to worry about prison.

Dillard looked around the boat's cabin. They had removed anything that could be used as a weapon, but they lacked his imagination. Everything could be a weapon to him, even the newspapers. It wasn't getting free and subduing the guards that had him worried; it was how to get Yarslova back and take possession of the trawler. He estimated that there were eleven Russians on board the trawler and two on the fishing boat, and his assets were four military-trained men, two women, and one untrained man. He'd had worse odds. He wasn't counting Yarslova.

Dillard had come up with a plan that he was only sharing with Dave and Tom. It was dangerous, foolhardy, and had only a slight chance of success. He knew that if he found a way to remove their guards up on deck, the soldiers on the trawler would notice and take action. His plan involved removing one guard at a time. Tom and Mike would put on their uniforms and, hopefully, fool the trawler personnel. However, removing the guards unnoticed was going to be a real feat.

The stern cabin window of the trawler faced the forward deck and pilothouse door of their fishing boat. The weather had turned colder, the fog thicker, and the trawler soldiers had gone inside to stay warm. The two guards on the fishing boat huddled together by the cabin overhang, trying to stay as warm as possible. Dillard figured that they would be relieved soon and two new soldiers would be sent over as guards. That's when they would make their move on the trawler. But first he had to disable the two guards.

The two men stood up. Dillard moved against Tom so he could get at his pocket. Dillard still had the penknife in his front pocket, but he was bound so tightly he couldn't move his hands enough to get at it. Tom would have to do it. He tried to position himself as close to Tom's fingers as possible. He knew the others in the group must be wondering what they were doing. He could feel Tom's fingers trying to get inside his pocket. He sucked in his breath to make the pants as loose as he could, and he felt the penknife being drawn out.

The next issue would be how to open it. The Russians had been careful to bind them with their hands apart, but they didn't bother with the women. When Tom had the knife, he whispered for Myrna to come over to him. She almost fell when a swell rocked the boat, but she made it. Leaning against Tom, Myrna took the penknife from him and pried open the small blade. She put it back in his left hand then sat down on the deck out of their way. Dillard moved against Tom again, this time with his back to him. Tom began sawing on the ropes.

Dillard had released all of the group. They stayed huddled together while Dave and Dillard worked on removing the portside window of the cabin. It wasn't easy; the window wasn't made to open, but the wooden frame had softened up from moisture over the years, and they dug at it with the penknife and a nail Dillard had pried out of the galley island. They had to be careful. Too much noise or seeing the window move would draw attention. Dillard had picked the port window because the fishing boat was slightly to the left of the trawler's stern. The swells kept increasing, which meant a squall was probably headed their way. For now, that was good, but if it got too bad, the Russians would move them all onto the trawler and sink or cut the fishing boat loose. Dillard had a short time frame.

The window was out; spray from the waves was coming into the cabin. The water would be cold, and Dillard's plan included him getting into the ocean and then climbing back on deck where the walk-around started. The walk-around didn't extend all the way to the aft of the fishing boat on the port side; only the scupper rail went all the way back. He knew he'd only have a few minutes to move through the water before the cold drained his energy. He was going to use the boat's scupper rail hand over hand through the water to the walk-around then pull himself up. He'd have to fight both the cold and the current of the moving boat.

The port walk-around ended about two feet past the back of the pilothouse. That two feet would have to be enough room for Dillard to pull himself up and squeeze in close to the cabin to keep from being detected by the trawler or the guards. The guards would be on the starboard side, huddled against the pilothouse. If he was lucky, they wouldn't hear him over the exhaust sounds of the trawler's twin diesels. Tom had volunteered, so had Dave; but it was Dillard's plan, and he trusted himself more than anyone. He knew they were worried because of his age, but it really wouldn't be a factor.

Dillard took off his boots, socks, and pants. Tom gave him an old T-shirt, and he slipped it on. Tom and Dave couldn't help noticing the scar tissue on his back and left shoulder. He was obviously fit; his muscles rippled as he donned the T-shirt. Tom felt better realizing Dillard was probably more fit than him or Dave. Someday, he'd like to learn more about the mysterious Dillard Ross.

Chapter 44

He eased himself out of the window, holding on to the sill and trying to grab the scupper. His bare feet weren't in the water yet, but they were already freezing from the icy spray and starting to go numb. That might be a problem when he tried to climb back onto the deck.

He grabbed onto the scupper rail with his right hand and let go of the windowsill. He held himself there then lowered his body into the moving water. It started knocking his body around at once, trying to rip his grip from the scupper rail. He hung on for dear life. If he got washed off, that would be the end. Hypothermia would claim him right away, and he'd sink like a rock.

Dillard started his hand-to-hand movement toward the front of the boat, his body buffeted by the waves. He had already lost feeling in his legs and feet. Foot by foot he pulled himself along the rail toward the front of the pilothouse. While it only took a few minutes, it felt like hours. He was at the spot where he needed to pull himself up, and now he wasn't sure he could. His 190 pounds wasn't a lot of weight, but it felt like he was trying to lift a thousand. An old piece of rope was attached to the side of the pilothouse. He grabbed it with his right hand and used it and his left arm to lever himself on top of the scupper rail. His feet were just above the waterline, and he pulled himself into a sitting position in the two-foot space. He sat there for a few minutes, hoping his circulation would begin to thaw his legs. His feet started to ache, telling him that feeling was coming back. The air was at least ten degrees warmer than the water, and he was beginning to get feeling back. He was still afraid to stand.

Dillard squirmed around and pulled himself up to his knees. His legs and feet were on fire, and his shoulders ached from the strain, but it made him feel alive. After about two minutes on his knees, he stood up, leaning into the cabin to keep from falling into the ocean. He was back in control of his body.

Dillard didn't even feel the cold spray and wind through the wet T-shirt. He couldn't hear the guards talking, only the diesel engines of the trawler. The fog had gotten heavy, and visibility would be bad in the trawler. He changed his plan. He would take out both guards, do the uniform change, and wait for the relief guards to be sent over. They would have to stop the trawler and pull the fishing boat alongside to board, and that's when Dillard, Tom, Dave, and Mike would attack the trawler. They'd disable the two new guards, take their weapons, and get on board the trawler. Dillard and Tom would go first, dressed in the original guards' uniforms. The soldiers on the trawler wouldn't realize who they were until they were on board. Mike and Dave would come right behind with the other guard's weapons.

Leaning there, Dillard thought to himself, *I'm too old for this shit.*

Dillard cautiously peered around the cabin. The two guards were huddled together, smoking and probably too miserable to even look his way. They were more interested in watching the trawler to see if their replacements were getting ready to relieve them. Dillard used their distraction to move around the cabin in their direction. He got within a few feet before they realized he was there. They didn't have a chance to raise their weapons before both were unconscious. He didn't feel the need to kill them, just disable them.

I'm getting soft in my old age, he thought, taking their weapons.

He moved slowly back to the pilothouse door and knocked softly. Tom opened it and took the weapons from Dillard. Mike came out on deck, and he and Dillard dragged the unconscious guards into the cabin. Dave started stripping the unconscious guards of their uniforms, and when finished, they were bound with the ropes that had secured Tom and Dave. Myrna used duct tape to tape their mouths.

Tom and Dillard now had uniforms on and carried assault rifles. The sidearms were given to Myrna and Dr. Evans. Dave and Mike would get the two assault rifles from the replacement guards and join Tom and Dillard on board the trawler. Now they just had to wait for the trawler to slow down and pull the fishing boat alongside.

Nothing happened for the next forty-five minutes. Suddenly, the exhaust note changed, and the two boats began slowing down. The trawler had to do it slowly to keep the fishing boat from running into them. Finally, both boats were stopped, and the guards on the trawler started pulling the two boats together. Dillard and Tom pretended to help secure the boats together. Finally done, the two guards on the trawler yelled at Dillard and Tom to be ready to come over after they came on board. Dillard waved "okay" at them.

The new guards jumped across. Tom had his back to them, supposedly watching the pilothouse door. Dillard was bending down, supposedly working with the ropes between the two boats. Both guards walked over to Tom and, speaking in Russian, told him to turn around and go back to the trawler. Tom didn't speak Russian but figured out what they wanted. There was another soldier on the trawler who was waiting for the first guards to come over. Then he would untie the boats and let the fishing boat drift behind them. He wasn't paying attention to what the guards were doing on the fishing boat.

Dillard got up and walked back to the new guards. One of them turned around to speak to him and realized it wasn't who he thought it was. He hit the deck, his assault rifle clattering on the wooden planks. The other guard spun around quickly, but Tom hit him with the butt of his rifle. He caught the guard's gun as he slumped down to the deck. The soldier on the trawler didn't realize what had happened and was still expecting the replaced guards to come on board.

"*Potoropis' vasiliy!*" the trawler soldier shouted to them. He couldn't see what was going on through the fog. He was telling Vassily to hurry up. Dillard turned and started over to the side of the boat where it was secured to the trawler.

"*Ya idu, ya idu,*" he called out with his head down. He jumped across the gap between the boats, putting his hand out for the soldier to help him.

As the soldier reached out, Dillard grabbed his arm and swung him into a turnbuckle, knocking him out. As he turned back to the fishing boat, Tom, Mike, and Dave all jumped the gap and were on the deck of the trawler with him. All were armed with assault rifles. He could see Dr. Evans in the open pilothouse door with her pistol out.

Good for you, Doctor, Dillard thought, turning back to the work at hand.

Chapter 45

They took possession of the trawler without firing a shot. The surprise was total, and they disarmed the trawler crew and locked them in one of the small cabins. He got the rest of the group from the fishing boat and untied it so it would tow behind. They were now underway, heading back toward Ukraine. Dillard knew they wouldn't be able to dock in Varna, and as difficult as it was going to be, he believed their chances would be better traveling through Ukraine to Chernivtsi and getting picked up by the United States. If that didn't work, they'd try for Poland rather than take their chances in Bulgaria, Belarus, or Moldova. He was sure that the trawler had radioed their position when they were picked up, and hopefully, the Russians wouldn't figure out that they had backtracked to Ukraine.

The Russians had been radioing the trawler constantly. Finally, Dillard said it would be better to answer than remain silent. He asked Yarslova to do it, but first, he went back to the cabin where the crew was being kept and got the names of the ship's captain and the radioman. Fortunately, their names were on their uniforms because they weren't being helpful. He wrote them down for Yarslova, who then called the Russian command ship. Yarslova knew how the radio protocol was supposed to go, so Dillard just stood back, motioning for everyone to be quiet.

"Russian Command Ship, this is the Russian trawler *Boslov*, Starshey Leytenant Yuri Buchanneski in command. Over." Yarslova was speaking in Russian.

There was static on the line, then a voice responded, "Starshey Leytenant, this is Kapitan Valadamir Chenkof of the Russian missile cruiser *Moskova*. Explain why we could not contact you. Over."

"Apologies, Kapitain Chenkof, we are having radio difficulties. Over."

"Status of your prisoners, Leytenant." They wouldn't say Putin's name over the radio.

"Sir, all prisoners are subdued and being held under guard."

"Good, Leytenant. Give me the coordinates of your . . ." There was silence on the radio.

Yarslova tried to reach the *Moskova* several times but just got static.

"Something has happened. I can't reach the *Moskova*," Yarslova said.

Dillard was puzzled. Knowing how important Yarslova was to the Russians, he couldn't understand why they suddenly went radio-silent.

"Okay, Yarslova, we'll try again in a few minutes. I know there is rough weather in Odessa Bay now, but that shouldn't bother a missile cruiser."

Yarslova put the transmitter down and moved away from the comm-set so Dillard could use it. He called Rossof on a frequency only he and Captain Rossof knew about. He described what had happened but left out most of the details: the attempted sabotage on the fishing boat and their capture then escape from the Russians. Then he asked Rossof to find someone who would drive the trawler and tow the fishing boat toward Odessa. Dillard said he planned to anchor offshore near the mouth of the Dniester River on the Moldova side and wait to be picked up.

He figured most of the Russian attention was to the south and west of them around Donetsk, Odessa, and Kiev. He thought their best chance was to drive from Odessa to Chişinău in Moldova, spend the night, then drive the fourteen hours to Warsaw, Poland. Moldova was being overrun with refugees from Ukraine, and they would have a good chance to blend in. Then he told Rossof that they had radioed the Russians to keep them thinking Yarslova was still their prisoner. He said that the communication had suddenly cut out and he didn't think it was on his end. Having made his report and requests, Dillard said he was signing off, and Rossof said he'd get to work on Dillard's needs.

It was late afternoon when the winds finally started to subside. It was hard to tell the time of day out on deck because the gray fog had never lifted. The trawler had good radar, and he was plotting their course to the river. They still hadn't been able to contact the *Moskova*, and it had not tried to call them again. Dillard put the issue aside.

Even though they couldn't see the mouth of the river, they could hear the waves breaking on the jetties. Dillard decided they were close enough to the mouth of the river and set anchor. Mike, Dr. Evans, Myrna, and her assistant went rummaging for food, and fortunately, the trawler was well equipped. They prepared a meal while Dillard, Tom, and Dave talked strategy.

Chapter 46

The small boat reached the trawler after dark. Dillard was surprised to see them plowing through the swells at well past 11:00 p.m. The boat wouldn't hold all of them, and he wanted to know how they planned to transport everyone to land. One of the three men told him that they were going to use the fishing boat tied in the back to take them to land then continue on toward Odessa. The other two men would stay on the trawler. He asked him what they were going to do about the Russian prisoners. He just looked at Dillard and didn't answer. Dillard went inside and told the crew to pack up; they were leaving.

It took forty-five minutes to dock the fishing boat in Moldova. Dillard and the crew, including Yarslova, got off and walked down the jetty to the public launch ramps. Even before they got off the jetty, the Ukrainian fishing boat had pulled out and was headed out to sea. Up ahead, Dillard saw a blue van similar to the one Sergi had driven them in. No one was around, but it wasn't locked, and the keys were in the ignition. The tank was full of gas.

Everybody piled in. As before, there were no back seats. Yarslova sat in front with Dillard; the rest sat anywhere they could. The trip to Chişinău should only take about three hours, but you never knew what might come up. He figured they had confused the Russians enough that they had a good chance of getting to Warsaw undetected. Moldova wasn't at war with Russia, but they had such a large influx of refugees from Ukraine Dillard was afraid that fuel and supplies might be hard to find. They had brought what food they could from the trawler, but fuel was another issue. They'd find a way.

The van had a map sitting on the dash with the route marked in red. He looked at it and started the engine. Yarslova was going to play navigator. They drove out of the Zatoka public launch area and got on R30 toward Chişinău. There was little traffic here. If there was going to be congestion, it would be from Chişinău on toward Poland. That's where the refugees would be entering Moldova to escape the Russians.

Dillard had read about Zakota. It is a popular beach community in the summer months, but now it was mostly deserted. Its claim to fame is the long beach area located on the Budzhak spit that separates the Black Sea and the Budzhak estuary. The rest of the village is situated on Karolina-Bugaz spit between the Black Sea and the Dniester estuary. It has quite a few inexpensive hotels, but now they were closed up. It was a beautiful little resort town, but this summer it would probably have to survive without the tourists.

Outside the area they were traveling through was a checkerboard of farmland. Dillard knew there were serious issues between Moldova and Ukraine because of the power plants being built on the western banks of the Dniester River. Both Ukrainians and Moldovans were experiencing water quality and quantity issues downstream of the power plants. The Dniester Basin in Moldova covers a major part of country's area with almost three million people living within its area. The Dniester River basin is Moldova's main source of drinking water for the population. But even with the hardships caused by the power plants, Moldova opened its borders to the Ukrainian refugees and welcomed them in.

They passed the town of Purcan, making good time on R30. It was around 2:00 a.m., so traffic was light. There were few reasons to slow down, and only when they came to the towns did Dillard take his foot off the gas. Time was critical, and he was in a hurry to get as far from Odessa as he could.

Myrna asked if they could pull over for a minute for a bathroom break. Apparently, more than one of the passengers had been crossing their legs. Dillard told Yarslova to watch for a wide spot, preferably with some bushes or trees. Within a mile, Yarslova told Dillard to pull into the wide spot they were coming up on. He did, and as soon as the van stopped moving, the side door slid open; several of his passengers headed out toward an old, deserted building. Dillard took this time to study the map. He figured they had about seventy miles to go. They'd get to Zakota too early to find a hotel. Hopefully, they could find a secluded place to rest up in Zakota before the drive to Warsaw. He still had three-quarters of a tank of gas, but he'd fill up in Zakota before heading to Poland. He made up his mind and got out of the van, walking a few feet away. The Ukrainians had given him a cell phone that could supposedly do overseas calls. He dialed Gabriele's number.

Chapter 47

Gabriele hadn't heard from Captain Rossof for two weeks, and she was getting worried. She had no way to get in touch with him, so she had to wait. Her family was concerned also, but they put on a happy face whenever they talked to her. The fact that he was in Ukraine during the Russian invasion scared them all.

She finished putting the groceries away. Lunch would be leftovers from last night's dinner, and the microwave dinged, telling her that the food was warmed up. She took out the covered plate, carried it to the kitchen table, and sat down. She wasn't really hungry, but she knew she should eat. The portable phone was lying on the kitchen table within easy reach. She was never more than a few feet away from it. Suddenly it rang.

Thinking it was her daughter, she picked it up and said, "Hello."

At first all she heard was static, then a welcome, familiar voice said, "I miss you too."

* * *

"Mom, what's up with you today?" her youngest said. Her mother had been acting strangely happy all day. It was nice to see her smile again.

"Dillard called, honey. He's fine and hopes to be home in a week or so."

"What? When did he call? Why didn't you call us and tell us?" She tried to look stern, but it wasn't working.

"Only you and your sister are to know. Apparently, there's some reason our government doesn't want anyone to know where he is."

Chapter 48

Dillard kept the van at a steady sixty miles per hour. The road was clear, but there were many access roads, and the chances of some old farm truck pulling out in front of them were high. It was dark but clear, the wind carrying the clouds to the coast.

He couldn't believe that he had called Gabriele on the cell phone. He wasn't worried about it not being secure. He had said nothing that could pin down their location, but the fact that in the middle of fleeing for their lives he had taken the time and risk of exposure to call his girlfriend—this wasn't him; he didn't lose focus. This was what other people did. At least he was smart enough to take the battery out of the cell phone and discard both of them. He'd find a way to contact Rossof when they got to Poland. He had kept the call short, minimizing the chance that the Russians would track the call. Still, it was a stupid move, but he wasn't sorry.

Dillard decided to get fuel in Ruseni off R30 before the road became R2. There were several small towns in the area, but it was still very rural, made up of dozens of small farms. He woke Yarslova up and told him they would be stopping. Two miles later, he saw the exit for Ruseni and took it. The town was just houses and two large stone buildings. He saw a sign that said "бензин," Russian for *benzin*, or "gasoline" in English.

He pulled over to the building, and Yarslova went inside. He came out a few minutes later with an old man. Yarslova was speaking to him in Russian and pointing to the gas filler. The old man nodded his head yes and went back inside. A few minutes later, the old man came out carrying a five-gallon can with a spout. He came over to the side of the van with the gas filler, opened it, and started pouring the gas into the van. When he had emptied the can, he closed the filler cap and put the can down. Walking up to Yarslova's window, he asked for payment. Five gallons of gas cost forty dollars, double the price from before the Russian-Ukrainian conflict. Only five gallons was available for purchase. Dillard gave Yarslova the money, and he paid the old man. The five gallons gave them about three-quarters of a tank.

They pulled back onto R30 toward Chişinău, and within a couple of miles, the road sign said it was now R2. This road would take them all the way through Chişinău, where they would get on M14, then several more roads until they got on M12, six hours from Warsaw. They would be crossing back into Ukraine near Lviv, but this area had been pretty calm.

Dillard knew R2 speed limit was ninety kilometers, or fifty-five miles per hour. He kept to the speed limit. They were starting to pick up traffic now that they were closer to work hours. It was still early and still dark. He knew they would be hitting slow traffic soon, but for now nothing was slowing them down. They came around a turn near a stand of trees, and the road stretched straight ahead.

Dillard didn't hear the shot, but the bullet went through the windshield and into his chest just to the left and above his heart. He jerked the wheel but straightened it quickly and stepped down on the accelerator. The second shot took out the right front tire, and the van careened off the road at sixty. They bounced through a ditch and up into a cornfield. Dillard fought the wheel to keep them from overturning, and they finally came to rest in the field, surrounded by dry cornstalks waiting to be cut down in the spring. Seconds later, he yelled, "Stay!" opened his door, and got out.

The team in the back of the van had been thrown around hard. Myrna was unconscious, and the rest had cuts and bruises, but no one was badly injured. Tom tried to open the van's side door, but it was locked. He told Yarslova to unlock it, but Yarslova wouldn't. He said Dillard had told them to stay in the van and that was what they would do. Angry, Tom glared at him, but he turned back to the other passengers to see if they needed help.

Dillard knew that they were in trouble. He didn't know how many men were searching for them, but it wouldn't be long before they found them. He was unarmed. They had left their weapons in Zakota, not wanting to get caught with them. He had to find the shooters before they found the van.

He was bleeding just above his left armpit, but he could tell the bullet had missed the bone. He ripped off the bottom of his shirt and shoved it up against the wound, hoping to slow the bleeding. The adrenaline rush counteracted the pain, so for now he was operational. He bent over and started walking in the direction he thought the shot had come from, trying to keep his head below the top of the dry cornstalks. He had left his nightscope in the van.

Dillard heard them before he saw them. He crouched down, estimating that they were about fifty feet away and would pass within ten feet of him. It sounded like two men. He felt around on the ground for something to use as a weapon but found nothing. He felt one of the cornstalks. It was rigid near the base. He bent one over, trying to break it off without making noise. He used his foot to help snap it off. He went rigid when the stalk cracked. Listening, he couldn't hear them moving any longer. He waited, breathing slowly. He could feel the slow trickle of blood leaking down his side. There! He heard movement again. They were still about thirty feet away and moving together. He broke off the small end of the stalk, leaving him with a three-foot shaft. The stalk was rigid, the bottom part jagged, and it would have to do.

Chapter 49

Boris had been a Russian soldier all his adult life. He had seen action during the invasion of Crimea, so he was considered a seasoned war veteran. Juris was just out of Spetsnaz training. He was the sniper that had shot Dillard and the van tire with a 7.62×54 mm round. He was the one Dillard was worried about. Russian snipers spent many years training—not just in learning to shoot, but in technical and physiological studies, teaching them to make focused, smart decisions. Generally, a Russian sniper would have spent seven to ten years learning his trade before being sent out on an assignment. He knew he might be dropped in hostile territory without backup and must use his wits to escape and survive. Dillard knew he would be harder to surprise than the other soldier, so he had to be taken out first.

The scrape of a boot told Dillard at least one of them was within fifteen feet and heading directly toward him. He knew it must be the soldier; the sniper was being careful not to make noise. Straining, he heard it, a soft scrape of rubber on rock. That was the sniper. Both men were still together, and that was their mistake.

He let the first man pass him just a few feet away from where he crouched. He waited for the sniper. He heard the cornstalks move as the second man came forward, staying about six feet behind the first soldier. Dillard waited until he was about a foot past him, then suddenly stood and attacked. The sniper had to turn back toward the noise, losing half a second in reaction time. That was all Dillard needed as he thrust the cornstalk into his right eye as hard as he could. The man cried out, instinctively reaching for the cornstalk. Dillard struck his windpipe with his knuckles using all his body weight to power it. The sniper went down.

He quickly dived back into the dry corn, lying flat on the ground. As he expected, surprise and fear made the soldier begin firing his AK-12 assault rifle in all directions, not caring if he hit his partner or not. He was using it on full automatic, spraying two-shop groups at 650 rounds per minute as fast as he could pull the trigger. Within a few seconds, the thirty-round clip was empty. As soon as he heard the click, Dillard jumped to his feet and attacked him. The soldier didn't have a chance.

Dillard sat down on the trampled ground, trying to catch his breath. His chest ached, and he could tell he had lost a lot of blood. He was running on adrenaline, and he was still mobile for now. He stood up, staggering slightly, and started heading back toward the van. He followed the trail of trampled cornstalk to the van. He called out, not wanting to surprise them. Yarslova opened the passenger sliding door. Dillard asked Tom and Dave to change the tire and Tom to take the wheel. They both got out and helped him climb in.

The day was starting to lighten up. In the back of the van, Dr. Evans could see the hole in his shirt, both front and back. He was soaked in blood, and he was obviously in great pain, although he was trying to hide it.

"What can I do to help, Dillard?" she asked him.

"I need two large squares of clean cloth to make pads and a long strip of something to bind them to the wounds," he said.

Evans motioned Myrna, who was conscious again, to move over and help her. Dillard heard material tearing, and in less than a minute, he felt the squares of cloth being put into his hand.

"Now I need you to place the squares of cloth against the wounds, front and back, then bind them with the strip." He handed back the squares. "Help me get my shirt off," he said, trying to raise his left arm up high enough to get the shirt off.

"Stop, Dillard, I have a knife. We'll cut the shirt off."

Mike got into the van and moved near Dillard. He started cutting the shirt off. In front, the shirt was stuck to the wounds where dried blood held it. Mike tried to pry it off as gently as he could, but Dillard couldn't help but cry out as the shirt finally pulled free.

They felt the van being lifted then lowered again after the tire was changed. They left the blown tire there in the dirt. Tom got in the driver's seat, and Dave got in the back and slid the door closed.

Dillard was sitting up, a wide strip of cloth wrapped around his chest and tied at the side. Blood seeped through the cloth front and back, but the pressure had slowed it down considerably.

"We need to get you to a hospital, Dillard," Dr. Evans said, looking at the bloody pile of rags they had cut off him.

"Sorry, Doctor, that's not an option right now. Our first priority is to get to Yarslova into Poland, then we'll worry about me."

She frowned and started to object, but then she just closed her mouth and said nothing.

Chapter 50

They got into town in the middle of workday traffic. Even with the Russia-Ukraine fighting, people still had to make a living.

There are many buses trying to make their way through the city, probably filled with refugees, Tom thought.

Yarslova was doing a good job navigating them through the busy streets toward M14. Dillard leaned against the van wall, conserving his energy as best he could. The bleeding had stopped, but he was weak. He ate some of the food they had packed and drank water. That would have to do for now.

Dillard was concerned that the Russians would try another hit when their team didn't radio in. He didn't know how to avoid them since there weren't too many side roads going to the Polish border. He was also worried about their proximity to Transnistria, a breakaway state loyal to Russia. Fortunately, they wouldn't be going there.

Ironic, he thought, *that when we cross back into Ukraine, we won't be that far from Vinnytsia, where this all started.*

They had pulled over on a side road for a break. Dillard checked the bandages on his chest. The skin around the wound didn't feel hot, so he didn't think infection had set in. Dr. Evans checked his back, same result.

"Lee, we have to change vehicles as soon as possible. I know the Russians will try again."

"You mean, steal a car?" she said.

"No, I'm thinking something more appropriate for our situation. We can't get it until we get back to Ukraine because it must be registered there. Ask Tom to come back here please, would you. Thanks."

She moved across the van to the front where Tom was leaning against the driver's door. "Dillard needs to talk to you, Tom."

He nodded and got up, moving between the seats to where Dillard was sitting. Dr. Evans got into the driver's seat to give them more room.

"What's up, boss? You okay?" Tom asked, kneeling down.

"I'm good, Tom. I told Lee that we need to change vehicles."

"Lee?" Dave asked smiling.

"Dr. Evans, smart-ass. We have to wait until we cross back into Ukraine, but I want you and Yarslova to keep an eye out."

"What are we looking for exactly?" he asked.

"A small school bus."

"Yarslova, how far to the Ukraine border?" Tom called to the front.

"Hang on, hang on," Yarslova said. "Looks like about forty minutes. The first town in Ukraine is Rososhany. We'll cross the border at Briceni."

"How big is Rososhany?" Tom asked.

"Looks like two or three thousand people," Yarslova replied.

"Good, see if you can find an address for a middle or high school."

Yarslova looked puzzled, but he tried searching on his iPhone. It took a while because of the spotty reception.

"Okay, I have an address. Starobulvarnaya Street, number 4." He wrote it down.

"So, Dillard, how do we get through the border crossing? Chances are, the Russians have people there looking for us," Dave said.

"We need to stop before we get to the crossing and send someone to check it out. Did you hear that, Tom? Once we cross the border, head for Rososhany and Starobulvarnaya Street."

"Got it," Tom said, called to Dr. Evans, and after she moved to the back, he took his place in the driver's seat.

They drove another five hours then switched drivers. Mike took the wheel, having been updated on stopping before they got to the border crossing at Briceni. The van was running low on fuel. They had enough to get to Briceni, but they would have to fill it there. Dillard had hoped they could make it to Rososhany, but Mike didn't think they could make it.

It was late afternoon when they neared Briceni. Mike kept a lookout for a place to hide the van. He saw an old barn about half a mile from the town and took the dirt road up to it. They drove around to the back and found that part of the wall was missing. There was enough room to pull the van in. When Mike turned the ignition off, they all turned to look at Dillard.

"Okay, Mike, feel like taking a walk?"

Mike nodded his head yes, and they started discussing how best to approach the crossing.

Mike saw that the border crossing at Briceni had one guard booth: one window for eastbound traffic going into Moldova and, on the other side, one window for westbound traffic going into Ukraine. There was no gate to block the road. He could see two Ukrainian police officers in the booth and a Ukrainian police car parked behind the booth. Mike watched for about an hour, making a note of how much traffic was passing through and how careful the officers were. He also noticed an unmarked pickup parked on the side of the road four hundred yards back toward Briceni. He could see shapes that looked like two men sitting in front. He was careful to stay out of view.

Mike returned to the van and told everyone what he had seen. The officers didn't bother Dillard, but the pickup did. They would have to immobilize it and the two guys on watch. He was in no condition to confront anyone, so the job fell to Tom.

The time was 5:00 p.m. The town wasn't big enough to have a rush hour, but a few cars came through going into Moldova. No cars approached in the west lane. It got dark at about six thirty, and they agreed it was best to wait. Tom was taking Mike with him since Mike knew the location of the pickup. They decided to approach it from the rear, staying out of sight of the mirrors. Hopefully, there wouldn't be any traffic.

Mike and Tom got to the booth without a problem. The few cars that had been coming from Birceni dwindled out. They quietly went around the booth, staying out of sight. Mike was in the lead, taking them off the road and into a beet field and working their way past the pickup. They didn't know if the guys in the pickup had night vision glasses, but they had to assume that they did.

Mike and Tom would wait in the field behind the truck and cross the road after a car went by. The lights would make their night vision equipment unusable and, hopefully, distract the two occupants. The one wrinkle was getting to the men. If they had locked the doors, Mike and Tom wouldn't be able to pull them open. Chances were that the pickup would alert the two police officers by honking or flashing its lights. Then they would have four people to deal with—that is, if the police officers and the guys in the truck were working together.

They sat in a ditch for close to an hour before a car finally came from Birceni. They readied themselves, and as soon as the car had passed the pickup driver's window, they crouched down and ran up to the truck, one on each side. Both men had knives, and they pulled the doors open at the same time, startling the driver and passenger. It was over in seconds.

Tom finished dragging the passenger out into the beet field. Nothing had alerted the men in the booth. They were Russian soldiers according to their identification. The men headed back through the beet field and then onto the road to the van.

Dillard didn't want to kill the Ukrainian police officers, but he couldn't have them radioing in, so Tom and Mike would subdue them, tie them up, and leave them in the booth.

Dillard hadn't thought about Birceni being on the border and that having residents from Ukraine and Moldova living there meant vehicles could be registered in either country. It was also a larger town than Rososhany, so there would be bigger schools and more buses to choose from. Yarslova had found a school close by, and they headed for it.

A dozen school buses were parked in the maintenance yard of the school. Dillard told them to look for a smaller bus, about an eighteen-passenger one. They were usually used for handicapped children or special events, but most schools, at least in the United States, had a few of them.

Dave broke off the metal clasp padlocked to the gate. All the buses would be locked, so they would have to find the bus administrator's office to get the keys.

Mike went looking for the office; Dave went looking for the right-sized bus. Mike saw Dave in the second row of buses. Mike didn't know which keys he would need, so he put them all in a box. Dave was standing in front of a smaller bus while Mike matched the bus number to the keys, and they unlocked it.

Inside there were seats for a dozen students. Dave switched on the ignition and saw that the tank was full. So far, so good.

Dillard and the crew waited inside the old van. Dillard had a shirt on that Mike had given him. He didn't ask where it had come from, but he couldn't miss the bloodstains near the collar. He was feeling stronger; the food and rest had helped his body replace some of the lost blood. He still wasn't ready for personal combat, but he was getting around much better. He'd let the others keep driving. They had parked the van a mile away from the school behind a deserted gas station. It shouldn't draw too much attention because it looked like a dozen other abandoned vehicles in the area. They waited for the bus.

Dave started the bus and turned on his parking lights. The diesel had fired up, and they pulled the bus up to the gate. Mike got out and opened it, letting the bus go through, and then closed it. From a distance, it would still look locked. No one would check until morning anyway. No, that was wrong; tomorrow was Saturday, and there was no school, so maybe they'd get a bigger lead on the Russians. Probably not, but Mike thought it was smart that Dillard had picked a school bus. It wouldn't look good on CNN if the Russians were shooting at a school bus, and Putin always thought about image.

He and Dave pulled up to the van, and the crew got in. They were relieved that it had seats; sitting on the floor was getting old. Dillard told Dave to keep driving, Yarslova changed seats with Mike, and they were off. Dave said they had fuel for about 280 miles, the bus not being much on economy. Yarslova started plotting the next fuel town.

Chapter 51

Dave drove up M12 toward Lviv. Once they reached the city, they'd fuel and then get on M10 all the way to Krakovets and the Polish border. Lviv was supposed to be relatively war-free, or at least it had been the last time Dillard checked. He'd contact Rossof once they reached the city.

The Moldova and Ukraine countryside looked similar, with small farms dotting the flat landscape. He knew that to the south the Carpathian Mountains rose to form a forest-steppe area and to the west it was highlands. Lviv itself was mountainous, so their pace would slow when they reached the grades. He knew the Russians would be waiting at the Polish border and Lviv, so the question was how to get past them. Once in Poland, Russia had much less chance of stopping them, and the US could intervene.

They were making good time in the little bus, but traffic was getting thicker the closer to Lviv they got. Refugees walked alongside the road headed for the city. Many of them would try to continue to Poland, which was less than fifty miles from Lviv. The bus didn't raise any flags because most of the schools' sporting events and field trips were done on the weekend. They continued on. Dillard was worried about running into a roadblock or road check. The Ukrainians were cautious, not wanting to let a bunch of Russian soldiers posing as immigrants into the city. His team had no official reason to be there and less reason to be driving a stolen school bus. If they were stopped, it would be an issue. He decided he'd better call Rossof.

"Captain, we are approaching Lviv in a stolen school bus. All of the team is intact." He didn't bother to tell him he'd been shot. "I'm concerned that we might run into a Ukrainian road check because of all the refugees trying to get into the city."

Rossof was silent for a moment. "How far are you from the city exactly?" he asked.

Dillard turned to Yarslova and asked him.

"Yarslova says twenty-five miles."

Again, silence, then he said there was a road check set up on M12 ten miles before the city limits. Then he asked for the bus number, the size of the bus, and the name of the school printed on the sides and back door. Dillard told him. Rossof said he'd get back to him.

They slowed done to forty-five while they waited for Captain Rossof's call. Yarslova's iPhone rang, and Dillard answered.

"Chief, whose cell phone is this?" Rossof said.

"Yarslova's, sir."

"We put a block on the phone number, but the Russians are probably trying to break into it now. As soon as we are finished talking, destroy it," Dillard said he would.

"I can get you safe passage through the checkpoints and the city, but after that, I can't do anything until you get to the border."

"That would be appreciated, sir. I have to stop for fuel. Can you tell me where that should happen?"

"Gas or diesel, Chief?" Rossof said.

"Diesel, sir." Again, Rossof was silent for a few seconds.

"Take the exit off of M10 for Silpo. It's about a mile off of M10. If you see the exit for the hospital, you went too far. I'll have people there to help. Get rid of this phone." The line went dead.

Yarslova put his hand out for the phone, but Dillard said, "Sorry, Yarslova," and handed it to Tom. "Crush it."

Tom did as asked. Yarslova started to say something, thought better of it, and turned back to face forward.

More and more people were lining the side of the road as they approached the checkpoint. Dave told Dillard that two police cars were on each side of the road and policemen were stopping everyone driving and walking. There was a line of cars waiting to be checked and waved through. The people walking had their own police officers checking their paperwork. Most had none but were let through if they didn't look like combatants.

The car in front of their bus was next in line. The driver was speaking to the police officer, but something must have seemed out of place because he blew a whistle and two more policemen came up, rifles pointed at the vehicle. The officer talking to the driver motioned him to pull over by one of the police cars. He was escorted by several armed police officers. They were next.

Dave pulled up to the police officer and stopped. He was told to roll down his window. The officer put his head in the bus and looked back at the passengers. He mumbled something and, stepping back from the bus, motioned Dave to drive on. Dillard could almost feel the relief of his team. They slowly pulled away from the checkpoint.

Dave made it to the Silpo exit without incident. He turned off M10 and drove to the village. The first business was a gas station, and they pulled up to the diesel pump. Dave started to get out, but a man dressed in coveralls told him his name was Joseph and for Dave to stay on the bus. He'd take care of the fueling. Within minutes their tank was full, and they were headed back to M10. Dillard made a mental note to thank Captain Rossof for his fast actions.

Back on M10, the traffic was heavy. The streets were still lined with refugees trying to get a ride to the border. Dillard was sorry he couldn't help them. They plowed on, never going over forty miles per hour. The border was less than fifty miles away, so they'd get there before nightfall. He didn't know how they'd get through the border crossing, but he trusted Rossof, who hadn't let them down yet.

Dave heard the honking before he saw the military truck passing the cars behind them. *Uh-oh*, he thought, *bet this is our welcoming committee.*

He told Dillard, who said he was surprised it took them this long to find them. He didn't sound surprised. Dillard got up and moved to the back seat so he could see out the back window. Dave asked him what they should do, and he said, "Just keep driving."

Dillard watched the approaching truck force a car off the road. They were still a dozen cars back but were coming on fast. He figured that when they were a little closer, someone in the truck would fire an RG-6 grenade or an RPG-30 rocket at them; at least that's what he would do.

"When I tell you, make a right turn off the road. It doesn't matter if there is a road there or not, just make sure you do it fast!" Dillard yelled to Dave. "The rest of you hang on to something because it's going to get really bumpy." He could see the fear in Myrna's eyes. "We'll be fine, Myrna. Just hang on."

She didn't look relieved at his words.

He watched the truck pass or force the other cars out of his way. They were only eight cars behind now, and Dillard knew they would be firing at them soon. They were desperate now, willing to take chances. He watched as it passed two more cars. Then he saw a man on the passenger side of the truck stick his head and shoulders out of the window and point something at them.

RG-6, Dillard recognized right away. Although it didn't have the stopping power of the RPG, it could fire multiple grenades instead of just one rocket.

"Now, Dave."

He felt the bus go up on two wheels as it made a right turn, going too fast. He jumped across the aisle to shift weight to the airborne side; Tom did the same. The bus hung there with its right wheels in the air then crashed down. Just as it did, they heard an explosion and saw cars slewing all over the road.

They missed this time, but it isn't over yet.

Dave was driving out across a farmer's field, dodging irrigation ditches and trees. The Russian truck was following behind, getting ready for another shot. The dust they kicked up helped obscure them, but it was just a matter of time.

"There, Dave, take that road. He saw a dirt road heading up a hill and turning right into a stand of trees. At least they would help block their shot."

"Turn left!" Dillard yelled, and Dave had the bus up on two wheels again. An explosion threw metal and rocks into the bus, breaking one of the side windows.

Dave whipped the bus to the right, and all the wheels were back on the ground. He headed up the hill toward the trees.

Dillard knew they couldn't keep this up. It was just a matter of time until a grenade got them. He was out of ideas. Suddenly a tremendous ball of flame erupted behind them. The truck was a pile of smoldering wreckage, and the Ukrainian MQ-9 Reaper drone turned away, headed back to where it was launched from.

Chapter 52

We are back on M10, shaken but not stirred, Dillard thought, though it was very uncharacteristic for him to think like that. *I must be getting old,* he mused.

They were within twenty miles of the Polish border near Krakovets. He didn't think the Russians could mount another attack fast enough to stop them unless they had something set up at the border itself. He doubted the Ukrainians or Poles would help them, and knowing Captain Rossof, he had already made sure of it. He looked out at the late-afternoon landscape. The Carpathian Mountains were off in the distance, and the farms had given way to rocky plateaus and streams cutting through wooded glens.

Beautiful country, he mused. *I'd like to bring Gabriele here . . .* He suddenly shook himself out of it. *This is how people die,* he thought. *You lose focus, you lose your life.*

He was back to reality: a stolen school bus with a broken window and nine people fleeing for their lives. He had a hole in his chest, and they still had huge hurdles to overcome to get to safety.

Dave could see the guard station up ahead. Dillard told everyone to stay calm. As they slowed down and stopped, several Ukrainian soldiers came out of the station, weapons trained on the bus. Dave and Yarslova raised their hands.

"Everyone step out of the bus," a PA suddenly called out.

Dillard told them to do exactly as they said. Tom slid the side door open and was faced with two more soldiers with assault rifles aimed at him and the others. Dave and Yarslova had gotten out and were herded to the side of the van with the rest of the group. The soldiers never took their guns off them.

An officer came out of the building, walking around the front of the van and over to the four soldiers pointing their guns at the group. In Ukrainian, he told them to lower their weapons. Then he faced the group and asked who Chief Ross was, and Dillard knew that they would be okay.

The Ukrainian guards escorted them thirty feet to Polish soil. Two soldiers with NATO armbands waited for them. As soon as they got there, the two NATO soldiers pulled Yarslova out of the group and led him to a parked car with diplomatic plates. It would be many months before Dillard saw Yarslova again.

A Polish officer came out of the guard station and asked them to follow him. They were led to another van, this one with seats and blacked-out windows. The officer closed the side door when they were all in and got into the front passenger seat. Not five words had been spoken.

They drove through the Polish countryside. It was rocky with granite plateaus like around Lviv, and the farms had given way to small rivers and patches of trees. Winter still had a grip on the country, although the snow was gone. Trees were still without leaves except for the pines. It was a beautiful, wild country. The Polish officer sitting in the front passenger seat turned and faced Dillard.

"We are not going to Warsaw. We are going to Krakow instead," he said in passable English.

"Is there a reason for the change?" Dillard asked him.

"Polish intelligence thinks the Russians might have tapped into Yarslova Putin's iPhone and heard Warsaw discussed. We are taking no chances. Mr. Putin will be flown out from a different location, and there is a US military transport at the air base in Krakow waiting for you." That was the end of the conversation until they arrived in Krakow.

Major Wojochowski had a medic patch Dillard up and give him a good dose of antibiotics. The wounds were healing.

The US Army C-17 Globemaster was parked by the maintenance hangar. It was hard to miss, being 174 feet long with a wing span of 169 feet, 10 inches. It was powered by four Pratt & Whitney F117-PW-100 turbofan engines. Dillard had to smile. This was typical overkill by Rossof. The plane could carry over one hundred soldiers and their equipment, so he figured his seven people wouldn't push it too much. Its unloaded range was approximately 2,400 nautical miles with a cruise speed of about 450 knots. Dillard figured they would be refueled in the air because the United States would want them back as soon as possible. He wouldn't be surprised that Yarslova was in the back seat of a fighter jet well on his way to the United States.

They boarded the plane and took seats near the front of the fuselage. Lee told him the plane was creepy because it was so big and empty. The three-man crew introduced themselves to the group. Dr. Evans was now considered in charge, and Dillard was happy to stay in the background. The pilot, copilot, and loadmaster said the trip would be relatively fast; they should be landing at Andrews Air Force Base in about twenty-three hours. Dr. Evans thanked them, and they went back to their duties. Less than an hour later, they were airborne.

There was quite a welcoming committee waiting for them. Dillard counted four staff cars. As soon as the plane had taxied up to a spot some distance from the airline passenger terminals, the engines were shut down and a ramp wheeled in place. The loadmaster opened the passenger door just behind the pilot's cabin and motioned for the group to deplane.

The group climbed down the gangway, a little worse for wear but happy to be back. They were ushered into the first two staff cars; Dillard was directed to the third. He opened the back door and saw Captain Rossof smiling at him.

"Welcome home, son," he said, putting his hand out to shake Dillard's.

Chapter 53

Gabriele had insisted on meeting him at the Jacksonville Airport. He was coming in on a regular commercial airliner, just like hundreds of others. They landed at 10:50 a.m., and there she was, waiting anxiously at gate A6. She ran into his arms, acting more like twenty than fifty. It hurt, but it hurt good, and he didn't shy away from the embrace. They headed for the exit, but she wouldn't let go of his hand, probably afraid he would disappear again. Her car was in short-term parking, and when they got to it, she said she was driving. He didn't mind.

"Jessie said your place is fine. Do you want to go there or my house?"

"Let's go to my place. I need a shower and fresh clothes."

"You stink, my love," she said, wrinkling her nose. They pulled out of the airport and headed toward St. Augustine on Highway 10. A while later, she took the exit for Highway 23 and headed toward Middleburg. Traffic was light, and they were making good time. Keystone Heights was sixty-five miles from Jacksonville Airport.

Dillard was happy to see the tropical splendor that was Northeastern Florida. It was still early in the year, and the summer heat hadn't set in yet. Outside it was a balmy seventy-six degrees with a slight breeze, almost identical to the weather he had left almost a month before. He rolled down his window and took a deep breath of humid air. He was one of those weirdos that actually liked humidity, and he seemed to be the only person in Florida that did, or at least the only person he knew that did. Fall, winter, and spring were wonderful times of the year in Florida; but he liked all the months, heat or not. It reminded him of many of the tropical places he had been in: Vietnam, Costa Rica, Cuba, and several others.

They turned onto Highway 100, and within two miles, they were at his driveway.

Gabriele turned down his hill and parked behind the Jeep. Dillard noticed that the lawns had been mowed and knew whom to thank for that. They got out and went through the gate to the main door of the house. She used the padlock and punched in the code. The door buzzed and opened. Inside it was cool and clean.

"I'll be out in a minute," he said and headed into the master bedroom to get clean clothes.

A few minutes later, she heard the shower running.

"Look, I know you can't tell me what happened over there, but you have to tell me something. You suddenly disappear to a foreign country for a month and come back with a bullet hole through your shoulder." She wasn't smiling now. They were lying in bed, the television on but not being watched.

Dillard cleared his throat. This was unchartered territory; he never had to answer to anyone before.

"All I can tell you is that I went to Vinnytsia to an archaeological site. My task was to check on the NATO archaeological team's security setup and give the security team some ideas. I wasn't there to get shot at. It just happened, and that wasn't even until we were on our way to Poland. I just happened to be at the wrong place, at the wrong time. It was an accident."

Gabriele was silent, which Dillard interpreted as not believing his story. He wasn't good at this.

"Forget it. Just promise me you won't disappear on me again. Can you do that?"

He promised, hoping he could keep it.

Dillard had been back for two weeks when he turned on the news one night to headlines saying, "Russia Suddenly Pulls Out of Ukraine."

The reporter went on to say that for some reason, Russia had suddenly ceased all military action inside Ukraine and was pulling their men and equipment out of the country. President Putin simply said that he was tired of the loss of life on both sides and had decided to iron out their differences through diplomatic channels. There was a huge uproar in Russia, one that might cost Putin his presidency, the reporter said. Dillard smiled; Yarslova must have come through.

He felt good, like something he did had actually made a difference. He wished he could share this with Gabriele, but that was out of the question. He wondered what else the United States might be able to pressure Russia into, because there was no doubt in his mind that was what just happened.

He took a sip of his Jack and Coke, thinking about what he had just heard, when his cell phone went off.

Probably Gabriele, he thought, smiling, but when he saw the number, his smile froze.

"Chief, I need you once more," the conversation started.

Rossof yelled into the phone, "I'm done, Rossof! I'm not available now or in the future. I won't do this to Gabriele again. Best of lu—"

"Shut up, Dillard, and listen to me. I need you and Gabriele to come to DC on April 4. The president of the United States requests your presence, and this is not a request you can say no to."

Dillard was silent.

Chapter 54

They boarded an American Airlines flight to Dulles International Airport. Captain Rossof had sent them first-class round-trip tickets along with a hotel reservation for the Four Seasons in Georgetown. They would be gone for four days.

Gabriele didn't know why they were going to meet the president, and for that matter, neither did Dillard. He'd received several "I'm proud of you, son" letters from two presidents and a handful of medals that were collecting dust on his desk. He wasn't sure what this was all about.

They landed at Dulles, and as soon as they got to the gate, a flight attendant came on the PA system and asked everyone to remain seated while they deplaned two VIP passengers. Both Dillard and Gabriele were embarrassed as they stood up and followed the flight attendant out of the plane to the arrival gate.

Waiting for them was Captain Rossof in full military splendor, wearing over thirty years of campaign ribbons and medals, including two Purple Hearts.

It is amazing he can remain standing up straight with all that brass, Dillard thought.

Rossof walked up to them and said, "Gabriele, it is my pleasure to finally meet you. Dillard, you told me she was beautiful, but not this beautiful." He kissed her hand.

Blushing, Gabriele smiled and thanked him. Dillard just groaned.

"Come on, kids. Our chariot awaits," he said with a flourish and took Gabriele's arm.

Kids, Dillard thought, *he'll never change.* They were dropped off at the hotel. Captain Rossof didn't get out of the car but said they had dinner arrangements at 7:00 p.m. and he'd send a car. Their luggage would be sent to their room.

Inside the hotel, Gabriele looked around, impressed with the surroundings. It was a regular haunt for diplomats and government VIPS, and it looked like it. Their room was a fifth-floor suite with a terrace. Standing outside, they had views of the C&O Canal, the Potomac River, and the rooftops of Georgetown. The private terrace included lounge chairs and a dining set. Gabriele's eyes were huge.

"Don't get used to it, sweetheart. It will probably never happen again." He smiled, enjoying her pleasure.

"Just who are you, Dillard?" she asked, only partially kidding.

"Obviously, they've confused me with someone else," he said, going back into the room and over to the complimentary champagne.

"May I offer you a glass of champagne?" he said in his best English accent.

"Thank you, sir," she said, coming into the room from the terrace. "You may deliver it to the bathroom. I'll be the naked one in the frothy bathtub."

They had dressed for dinner. He didn't know what this was about or whom they would be dining with, so to be safe, he donned a suit. He left off the tie. Gabriele was dressed in an A-line scoop neck chiffon dress. Dillard didn't know what that meant, but she looked incredible, and he wasn't the only one who noticed.

They waited in the lounge for their car. He saw a black SUV pull up. *Wow*, he thought, *stereotyped*.

They went out the door. The driver had gotten out and was holding the back door open for them. Inside it was at least two and a half cows' worth of leather. They settled back in the plush seats, and the driver pulled out into the DC traffic. Dillard was at once reminded of why many residents got rid of their cars when they moved to the city. Driving was next to impossible, and the Metro went everywhere.

They turned east on Pennsylvania Avenue NW toward Twenty-Eighth Street. At Washington Circle, they took the third exit and stayed on Pennsylvania Avenue. The driver turned left onto H. Street and then right on Fourteenth Street NW. He turned left at the second cross street onto G. Street NW, and the restaurant was on their right. The driver pulled up by the front door, turned off the ignition, and got out to open their door.

"Is this how you always travel, Dillard?" Gabriele asked, obviously impressed.

"Not even close, sweetheart," he said, turning to thank the SUV driver.

"I guess we just go inside and see what's waiting." He took her hand, and they went through the main door and up to the reservation desk.

"Hello, my name is . . ."

"Oh, no worries, Mr. Ross, we are expecting you."

Gabriele turned to look at him, and he shrugged his shoulders.

"Please follow me." She stepped from behind the kiosk, and they followed her into a crowded dining room, past the busy diners, and to a private dining area.

Inside more than a dozen people were seated. They stood and clapped when he and Gabriele came in. Captain Rossof was at the head of the table, dressed in civilian clothes this time. He indicated two empty places, one on each side of him. They came in and sat down.

"Gabriele, I know it isn't fair that you have no idea what your man has done for our country. These people here wouldn't be sitting here tonight if it wasn't for Dillard. You are going to hear things tonight that might upset you, but try to remember, everything that happened was so that the United States and its allies could find a way to stop the killing of thousands of innocent people in Ukraine and, hopefully, prevent it from happening again."

"But I thought—"

"Dillard wasn't allowed to tell you the truth, Gabriele. It wasn't his fault. It's just the way it works in the US intelligence community."

She frowned and looked at Dillard.

"It won't happen again, Gabriele," he said.

"It won't happen again, Gabriele," Captain Rossof echoed.

That night Dillard told her everything about the Ukraine trip, and he held nothing back. He was afraid—afraid she wouldn't be able to deal with some of the things he had done—but he underestimated her. When he was done, the only thing she said was, "It won't happen again."

Chapter 55

The SUV was at the hotel on time. Dillard wasn't surprised; after all, they were on their way to meet with the president of the United States. Gabriele was nervous but beautiful in a white satin gown that showed off her golden-brown skin. Dillard was decked out in a black-and-white tuxedo, the second time in his life he had worn one. The clothes had been provided by Captain Russof.

They drove across town and up Pennsylvania Avenue again, only this time they were headed to the White House. He could see buds on the cherry trees, further testimony that spring was near. The weather was cool, fifty-eight degrees with a slight breeze. Not uncomfortable, but they wouldn't be outside much anyway. Apparently, tonight's festivities included a hosted dinner.

They were ushered through several checkpoints and into a private entrance on the east side of the grounds. When they stopped, several Secret Service agents checked their credentials against the electronic datasheets they had on their cell phones. They also checked thumbprints and did a retina scan. This was the most intense screening Dillard had been through, and for Gabriele, it was a little disconcerting. They followed the agents into the West Wing of the White House. Gabriele moved left and right as she tried to take everything in.

Dillard and Gabriele were asked to wait in a lounge area outside the Oval Office. A naval officer approached them, saluted Dillard, and told them that they would be meeting with the president, his chief of staff, his press secretary, and the chairmen of both the House and Senate. Rear Admiral Thompson, the secretary of Defense and the director of the Central Intelligence Agency, would join them for dinner, which would be prepared by naval culinary specialists and served in the White House Mess, a small restaurant run by the Presidential Food Service.

Gabriele was awestruck. *Who is this man?* she thought as she looked at Dillard, who appeared calm and uncaring.

They were ushered into the Oval Office. Gabriele noticed the portrait of Franklin D. Roosevelt above the ceremonial fireplace. She knew that depending on the president's party affiliation, the portrait would be either Franklin D. Roosevelt or Theodore Roosevelt. In President Freemont's case, he elected to keep Franklin D. Roosevelt's portrait even though he was a Democrat.

Gabriele looked around at the Oval Office. It was as beautiful as it had been described. The first lady had it decorated with articles from past presidents' tastes, such as the Resolute desk, which was made from the oak timbers of the British ship HMS *Resolute* and given as a gift to President Rutherford B. Hayes from Queen Victoria in 1880. It had been used by US presidents since Hayes, except for Presidents Johnson, Nixon, and Ford.

The drapery and navy-blue rug were from President Clinton's era, and the cream-colored sofas were from the George W. Bush collection. It was a beautiful room that radiated power.

Bill Davis, chief of staff for the president of the United States, walked up to greet them. He shook hands with Gabriele then Dillard as he introduced himself. He started explaining what was going to happen.

The ceremony would be over quickly, a proclamation read by the secretary of Defense that highlighted the importance of the award and also listed the many other awards Dillard had earned in the military. Dillard was presented with the Presidential Medal of Freedom by President Freemont, who offered it on behalf of a grateful nation. Bill Davis had explained that normally the ceremony would be done publicly with a lot more fanfare, but in this situation, it was limited to those who had a need to know. He apologized.

The medal itself was in the form of a golden star with white enamel and a red enamel pentagon behind it. The central disk had thirteen golden stars on a blue enamel background within a golden ring. A golden bald eagle with open wings stood behind the points of the star.

At the conclusion of the presentation, Dillard would be personally thanked, and his hand shaken by all those present in the Oval Office, Republican and Democrat.

The White House Mess was decked out with white tablecloths and blue-and-white china with the presidential seal on them. Dillard was seated next to Captain Rossof on one side and the president on the other. Gabriele was seated next to the first lady, with Dr. Lee Evans on her left. He was glad that Dr. Evans had been invited. He knew it was quite an honor for her to be here.

A dozen conversations were taking place at the same time. President Freemont was relaxed and friendly. He and Dillard talked about fishing and boats. No work conversations were allowed. Dinner lasted three hours, and then everyone was ushered out. They caught their ride back to the hotel after saying good night to the president and the first lady. Rossof was nowhere to be seen.

Chapter 56

The two men lounged on the red vinyl seats of the Four Winns. They were hoping for redfish but didn't really care if they caught anything. It was more of a "getting to know you better" kind of day.

Yarslova got another beer out of the cooler, and Dillard passed. He knew better than to try to keep up with Yarslova's drinking. Eight months had passed since they had fled Ukraine. The region was stable, and many countries were helping them to rebuild from the devastation left behind by the Russians. Putin was still president but no longer popular. It was assumed he would be voted out in the next election.

On the outside, relations between the United States and Russia seemed normal, but *normal* just meant they weren't shooting at each other. The public had no idea what was going on behind the scenes. Russia had restarted their cooperative space program with the United States, and there were even talks of other joint projects. The threat of nuclear war was distant. All in all, it was a relatively peaceful time.

Yarslova got a bite on his line and dropped his beer. Dillard was afraid he was going to jump in the water after the fish because he was so excited. It was ironic that a hard case like Vladimir Putin could have a son as good-natured as Yarslova—or Peter, as he was known here. The Russians were no longer trying to get to him, or so the US intelligence folks believed. Any information he had was already in the hands of the United States, so what was the point? The damage had been done. However, he could never go back to Russia, or his life would be forfeit.

Dillard knew Yarslova was feeling the beers. It was seven to two in Yarslova's favor. He was enjoying his freedom, or his perceived freedom. Dillard knew that the US government had him under surveillance at all times but was giving him some leeway since he was with Dillard. He had spent the weekend at Dillard's house, enjoying the lake and now a boat cruise down the St. Johns River.

"So why is the beautiful Gabriele not with us?" he asked Dillard.

"She and her youngest daughter are in St. Augustine shopping," he said.

"Aw, yes, the beautiful Emily, daughter of the beautiful Gabriele. I am surrounded by beautiful people. You, too, Dillard are beautiful." He beamed drunkenly.

Dillard remembered the long looks between Emily and Yarslova. That would have to wait until Yarslova was really out of the woods. Not that he didn't believe the intelligence boys; it's just that his nature was to err on the side of caution. This was, after all, the son of the president of Russia.

"Sorry, my friend, it's just you and me this weekend."

Chapter 57

Yarslova—or Yari, as his mother Patricia called him—had just turned six. He was having a birthday party, but the only guests were his mother and two men that worked for his father. He sat at the table, and his mom said he could open his presents. He was used to doing things without anyone his own age around, so he wasn't disappointed; he was used to it.

The card had the Russian seal on it. It was from his dad. He opened it, hoping for something personal, but it was just a typed card wishing him a happy birthday and signed by Vladimir Putin, prime minister of the Russian Federation. For a moment he was sad, but he moved on, not wanting to upset his mother. There were presents from uncles, aunts, and cousins, none of whom he had ever met.

Since he was born, he had been kept secluded. Even in the private school he attended, he wasn't allowed to interact with the other children, and they were forbidden to speak to him. All the students were children of high-ranking Russian officials.

Yari finished opening the presents. He thanked his mother and looked over the stack of toys and books he had been given. He picked up a book on Russian history and asked his mother if he could go out to the screened patio and read. It was a warm day, and like most six-year-old boys, he wanted to go outside. He had no interest in the book; he just used it as an excuse to go outside. Useff, one of his guardians, said he had something special for him. His mother looked surprised then thought maybe Vladimir had sent something special—or, though she didn't really believe it, maybe he had come to wish his son a happy birthday. She followed them out expectantly.

A black SUV with darkened windows was parked in the driveway, and Useff walked over to the back door and opened it.

Patricia could see someone sitting inside but couldn't see who it was. Yari went over to the car, thinking his father might be inside, but when he looked inside, he didn't recognize the man. Suddenly, Useff shoved him into the SUV and closed the door. Patricia cried out and started to run to the car, but Petra, the other guardian, grabbed her and held her back. The SUV pulled out, and Yari never saw his mother again.

* * *

Yari was sixteen. He had just finished his middle year at the General Yermolov Cadet School, and he'd be here one more year then transfer to the Russian General Staff Academy in Moscow. He was looking forward to it. Unlike the private schools he went to when he was young, here he could interact with the other cadets, play sports, and learn more about the world outside Russia. Of course, the view of the outside world was heavily modified to show the decadence and evilness of the Western world compared to the upright and honorable Communist world. But like most kids of Yari's age, he had found ways to get on the internet and get less-sanctioned points of view.

Now that he was sixteen, his father had shown more of an interest in him. He even let him visit the Kremlin, and Yari had met some of his father's associates. He didn't care for them much. They seemed cold, stuffy, and uptight, and they deferred to his father on everything. But then his father was also cold, stuffy, and uptight. His father never told him what had happened to his mother, just that she had moved abroad. In later years, Yari would learn that what his father told him was actually true, but he left out the reason she left.

Yarslova was a good student, excelling in sciences and math. He became a history buff and was fascinated with Russian history, up to and including the present day. His problem was that the more he learned, the less he liked modern Russia. Although the czars had been bloodthirsty rulers, there was some reasoning behind their atrocities. His father was more like Stalin. He sometimes made decisions on emotion, especially if it involved his image. The more Yari learned about his father, the less he liked him.

He was smart enough to keep his personal thoughts to himself. He had no confidants, no close friends to confide in, so he kept everything inside. As he grew older, his father began pulling him into his world more and more. He seemed to have a need to share things with his son, things that Yari should never have heard. He knew this was his father's way of getting him to respect him, but it didn't work.

While Yari showed appreciation and sometimes—when appropriate—awe about his father's achievements, inside he was shocked and horrified by Vladimir's disdain for the Russian people. In time he grew to hate his own father and got determined to put an end to his tyrannical ways. He learned anything and everything he could about his father, his secrets, his fears, and his plans for the rest of the world. When Vladimir Putin declared war on Ukraine, Yari knew he had to leave and get to the only country powerful enough to stop his father, the United States.

Chapter 58

Dillard reeled his line in and told Yarslova—*No, I must remember it is now Peter*, he thought—that it was time to head back. Yari pulled up his line. Dillard fired the Johnson Outboard up, pulled up the anchor, and started back up the St. Johns River toward Green Cove Springs. Yari sat back and opened another beer.

The cruise back up the river was pleasant. It was getting pretty warm now, spring was over, and summer was almost here. Dillard was sitting under the canopy while Yari sat in the back in the sun. He seemed to enjoy the sun and wanted to soak as much as he could.

No problem, Florida has lots of it, Dillard thought.

"Captain," Yari said, "do you think we could stop for just a minute so I could swim? I haven't done that for many years, and I would like to enjoy this warm day and warm water." He was smiling foolishly.

Dillard thought about it. Yari was pretty drunk, but the water would probably help clear his head. There was really no reason not to let him, so Dillard turned the boat toward the mouth of Trout Creek, about a quarter mile away. He stopped the boat a good distance from the creek entrance and told Yari to have at it. He got out a rope and float ring just in case and watched Yari climb up on the transom and jump or fall in. He surfaced, spitting water and looking happy.

"Come on, Dillard, come swim with me!" he yelled, splashing around happily.

Dillard could see he was a good swimmer, so some of his concerns lessened. *Why not*, he thought.

He tied the rope to a turnbuckle and tossed the float ring out of the boat. They weren't anchored, so the boat would drift. The float ring would keep them within range of the boat. He took off his shirt and dived off the transom.

The water felt wonderful. He and Gabriele had gone swimming off the Four Winns several times. After the first time, Dillard had realized he would need to add a boarding ladder because it had been too hard to get back in. Now it was easy. He swam around a little, keeping the float ring within easy reach in case they needed it. The boat was drifting slowly, and both men stayed close to it. After a few minutes, they were both ready to get back in.

He fired up the Johnson again and pulled the float ring back into the boat. They started back toward Green Cove Springs where he had left the Jeep and trailer. Yari was definitely more sober now and was just sitting back, enjoying the ride. They crossed under Shands Bridge headed for the landing. Pulling up to the dock at Shands Landing, Dillard told Yari to get out and catch the bow rope. He did and pulled the boat against the bumpers. Dillard shut the motor off and climbed up on the dock.

"Just hang on to it while I get the trailer," he told Yari and walked down the dock to the parking area.

Within a few minutes, the boat was on the trailer, and they were driving the twenty-five miles back to Keystone Heights.

"Are you hungry, Yari?" he asked.

"I would like some of that fast food. It tastes different than what we have in Moscow."

"Any preference on restaurants?"

"There is a McDonald's near your house. How about that one?"

"McDonald's it is."

They took their burgers back to Dillard's house and ate them in the screened porch, looking out at Paradise Lake.

"I envy you. Such a wonderful place, my friend," Yari said between bites.

Dillard realized then that they had actually become friends. He didn't have many.

"Yes, and now that I've found Gabriele, life is very good."

"So no more secret trips to save the world?" Yari asked.

"No, no more secret trips. That part of my life is done."

They finished eating in silence, each of them lost in their thoughts. Dillard realized it was almost 6:00 p.m. and decided he should check in with Gabriele. Yari would be leaving tomorrow, back to DC to make plans for his future as a US citizen. He picked up his cell phone, got up, and walked out onto the deck to call. He dialed her number, and it rang four times then went to voice mail. He left a short message and went back in and sat down.

They watched the sun get lower, and Yari told him about his childhood and growing up with a father like Vladimir. Dillard wasn't much of a sharer, but he was a good listener. After an hour, he got up and went back out on the deck to call again. Again, voice mail. That was a little strange, but Dillard wasn't alarmed. She did have a life outside theirs.

The two men went inside the house. Dillard made them both iced tea, figuring they'd done enough alcohol for the day. He could tell Yari was getting sleepy—not surprising after a day of sun and beer. Yari wanted to watch the news, and Dillard turned it on. The headline news was talking about some of the new reconstruction projects in Ukraine and the coming elections in Russia. There were rumors that Putin wouldn't run, probably because of his drop in popularity. But as Yari said, whoever did run in his place would just be his puppet. There was nothing else of note on the news, and they decided on an early night.

Dillard called Gabriele again at 9:30 p.m. Again, no answer. Now he was getting a little concerned. He put the phone down, deciding to drive over to her house just to check on her. His phone rang.

"Dillard," he answered, not recognizing the caller's number.

"It's me, Dillard. I'm in trouble," the familiar voice said. "Two men came to my house. They tried to get me to go with them. They had accents. Russian, I think. I locked myself in the bathroom and called 911, and when the police got there, they were gone. I'm scared, Dillard."

"Location now?"

"I'm at Emily's apartment."

"I'll be right there. Lock everything up, turn out the lights, do not stand in the window." He hung up and went out and opened Yari's bedroom door.

"They're coming for us, Yari. We have to leave now."

He turned around and went back into his bedroom, getting out the gun case under his bed. He took out the SIG Sauer P226 and extra clips and another pistol for Yari. He left the assault rifle, not wanting to get stopped with it in the car. He could hear Yari out in the living room. He went out, got two bottles of water, and told Yari to meet him in the Jeep.

"Be careful, Yari. We might have company."

Yari nodded and took the Colt M1911 pistol Dillard handed him. He'd call Rossof from the car.

Yari was in the passenger seat, pistol out. Before Dillard got in, he walked up the hill to the road, looking both ways for parked vehicles. He saw no one. Going back to the Jeep, he opened the driver's door and looked out at the lake. The moon was full, and the light glistened off the water. It also glinted off something across the lake in the trees.

Sniper, Dillard thought, yelling for Yari to get down.

Seconds later, a bullet hit the driver's door, but there was no sound of a report. Silence. He quickly got in, being careful not to give the shooter a target. He started the Jeep and, keeping the lights off, started backing up the hill. His door was still open. Another round hit the Jeep, punching a hole through the windscreen where the driver's head would normally be. They were up the hill and into the trees before the shooter could get off another shot. He closed his door and punched the throttle, the Mercedes 3.0 turbocharged diesel pushing the Jeep forward. The Grand Cherokee flew down the dirt road toward Highway 26. He half expected a pursuit vehicle but saw no one behind them.

There were several ways to get to Emily's apartment. Dillard chose to go through the town of Palaka then up the coast toward St. Augustine. He normally took Highway 16 to Gabriele's house, but he thought he'd better go a different route. Less chance of a welcoming committee.

He voice-dialed Rossof. He told him what was going on. Rossof was surprised; they had no warning of any follow-up action on Yari or him, so they were caught off guard. The agents assigned to watch over Yari were off for the night because he was with Dillard. They had gotten too complacent. He promised to mobilize help and meet them at Emily's apartment.

Dillard sped down the road. Yari was silent, watching intently for vehicles that might prove an issue. His military training was coming in handy. Dillard wasn't worried about being stopped by some local sheriff for speeding. This was a pretty rural part of Florida, and there weren't many policemen in the area. He kept the Jeep at a steady ninety; the road was long and straight.

When they got to Palaka, Dillard slowed, going through town. Outside town, he hit the gas again and ignored the forty-five-mile-per-hour signs. Still no sign of pursuit. He knew it wouldn't take them long to find Emily's and her sister's addresses.

Gabriele had called her oldest daughter, telling her to take the family to a hotel for the night. She knew Rossof would know what was going on by now and get security for her family. She needed Dillard.

Chapter 59

For someone who had never had to deal with something like this, Gabriele was doing amazingly well. Rossof's people had gotten Gabriele's daughters, granddaughter, and son-in-law safely out of harm's way.

The intelligence services were going through all communications intercepted during the past two weeks to try to find a link to the attack. They assumed it was Russian and was retaliation for Yarslova's defection and Dillard's rescue, but they couldn't find any information regarding the action. Agents had combed the woods across Dillard's house, but there was nothing. They were professionals. Yarslova was quickly picked up and transported to a secure site somewhere.

Gabriele looked out of the hotel window, wondering again how something like this could happen here in the United States. She was thankful that everyone was okay and that she was with Dillard, but she was still angry that someone had tried to kill him. Neither Rossof nor his team could convince her that it was okay now. She was no dummy. If those people had found his house, her house, and her children's homes, then they had local resources and were still a danger. The fact that nobody even knew who they were bothered her a lot.

"Let's take a little vacation, just you and me," Dillard said from the bathroom.

She thought about it. "I'll need to check with work. I have the time built up, but I need to see how busy they are. What are you thinking?"

"Mmm, someplace nice. You know, I've never taken a real vacation, but I guess being retired is supposed to be a full-time vacation."

"Not in your case, buddy," she said smiling. She didn't really feel like taking a vacation, not after last night, but then she thought about it. Perhaps it would draw any danger away from the kids, so feel like it or not, it might be a good idea. She didn't buy Rossof's statement that the assignation attempt had failed so they had packed up and gone home. She didn't think Rossof believed that either.

Dillard came out of the bathroom dressed in a towel. His gray hair was still wet from the shower, and he smelled soapy. She looked at him appreciatively. He caught her look and smiled.

"You know, we don't have to be anywhere for quite some time." The towel hit the floor.

Chapter 60

Saint Martin in French and English is also known as *Sint Maarten* in Dutch. It is a beautiful island. Being half French and half Dutch, it is a curious mix of cultures, especially when you add in the local population. Nestled between the Atlantic Ocean and the Caribbean Sea, it sits about 190 miles east of Puerto Rico. Hurricane Irma had devastated much of the island in 2017, but most of the hotels and homes had been rebuilt.

They were dropped off at *Hotel L'Esplanade* in Grand Case, Saint Martin. Perched on the hill above the village of Grand Case on the French side of Saint Martin, it looked down on Mediterranean-style architecture and the turquoise waters of the Caribbean. Just minutes from the town's gourmet restaurants and shopping, there was no need for a car.

Gabriele inhaled a deep breath of tropical air. Standing out on their private balcony, she was again amazed at how much the US government was willing to spend on keeping Mr. Ross happy. All this was on some government expense account that seemed to have unlimited funds. She almost felt guilty—that was, until she thought about the attack just two weeks ago.

Dillard was sitting in a lounge chair next to her. He was reading all the tourist info that they had left in the room: brochures on tours, shopping, restaurants, beaches, and anything else a happy tourist might spend money on.

Dillard is funny, she thought. *He's never been a tourist, and he is embracing it completely—well, almost completely, except for the gun I have seen in his luggage and the SAT phone sitting next to it.*

They didn't have to worry about customs; all that was taken care of for them. They just flew into the airport in Puerto Rico and were walked through Customs and straight onto the plane for Saint Martin.

"Honey, listen to this," Dillard said excitedly. Then in French, he continued, "*Chez Ginette, super cuisine avec un accueil à la créole et une patronne vraiment extraordinaire des saveurs en bouche et de la couleur dans la vie.*" Dillard looked at her expectantly. "Great reviews, five stars. They offer French, Caribbean, Cajun, and Creole food."

"Well, I don't know what the French means, but you make it sound yummy." *This guy is the hard-nosed soldier that the government is so thrilled about?* she thought to herself. *If Rossof could see him now.* She laughed to herself.

After three days, Dillard's enthusiasm was beginning to lessen. He could only eat so many big meals without it coming back to haunt him. He was running five miles each morning, but that and swimming a few miles each day just weren't enough to counteract coconut shrimp, lobster thermidor, and a multitude of spicy Creole rice dishes each day.

"Honey, let's do something different today," he said to Gabriele on Thursday morning.

"What do you have in mind?" she said. She was also getting tired of the rich food and too-lazy days.

"We could take a tour of the Dutch side of the island. I read that Philippsburg is a good town to walk in. I'm curious about the cultural differences between the two sides of the island."

"Yes, but a guided tour? Aren't they paid to just take us to certain businesses who compensate them for it?"

"Yeah, I read that too, but I'll find us one that will do what we want, not what they get paid extra to do."

Good luck with that, she thought.

Dillard went down to the front lobby to talk to the concierge. He explained what he was looking for, and she said she had just the perfect guide for them. She sent him out front and over to a shiny Mercedes eight-passenger transport. Strike one. The guide got out dressed in a toothy smile and designer Hawaiian shirt. Dillard told him what they had in mind, and he immediately said he knew just the right places to take them. He guaranteed Dillard that they had the best prices.

Dillard looked at him and said, "No, we aren't shopping. We just want to look around."

The guide nodded his head that he understood. Then he said they should start with Braxtons Jewelry in Philippsburg; his wife was sure to find something beautiful to remind her of this wonderful vacation. Dillard just shook his head and walked back inside the lobby while outside the guide kept up his pitch on the great shopping places only he knew about.

He stood in the lobby for a few minutes and watched a beat-up taxi pull up to the entrance. The driver hopped out and came around, opening the back door for his passengers. Two Europeans, a man and a woman, got out laughing.

"Hodge, you are a trip," the man said to the driver, smiling broadly.

"We haven't had this much fun in years, Hodge, thank you," the woman said. "Are you available next week for another tour?"

"I must check my agenda," Hodge said, looking at his hand. "Yes, it seems I'm free. Just call me at the number I gave you and think about what you want to see between now and then." He smiled, and they shook hands.

The Europeans came inside the lobby.

"Excuse me," Dillard said to the man. "I noticed you just got done with an island tour. My wife and I are thinking of hiring a tour guide for the day, but they all seem to want to take you to certain shops, not really tour the island. Do you have any recommendations?"

He looked at his wife. "That guy out there." He pointed to Hodge still standing by his taxi. "If you really want to see the island, hire him. You'll see places tourists don't normally see, and he will make it a fun time."

Dillard thanked him and went back outside. "Excuse me, I'm looking for a tour guide for tomorrow."

Hodge turned around and looked at Dillard. Hodge was a slim African American with a thin goatee and short dreadlocks. His T-shirt was clean, but not from some boutique, probably a Kmart that had a store on the island. His shorts and shoes were clean but well worn. His teeth, when he chose to smile, were white against his dark skin.

"Yeah, mon, I can do that. You tell me what you want to see, to do."

Dillard smiled back. "I'm not really sure. I just don't think we've seen the best parts of the island, the ones that tourists don't normally go to."

Hodge looked at him carefully. "Are you sure, mon? Sometimes those places aren't so pretty up close. You okay with dat?"

"We're okay with that," Dillard said.

"I get you at ten o'clock tomorrow. Wear good walking shoes but no fancy jewelry."

"Why don't we start a little earlier, say, eight o'clock?" Dillard said.

"No, mon, you in Saint Martin now. Nobody get up early here." With that, he turned and walked around to the driver's side of the taxi.

"See you tomorrow," he called out, smiling and waving. He got in his cab and drove away.

Then Dillard realized he hadn't even told him his name, but Hodge was driving off. *Well*, he thought, *I guess it doesn't really matter.*

Dillard told Gabriele about the highly recommended Hodge, who was going to be their tour guide tomorrow. She wasn't too sure how tomorrow would go, but she was game if he was. That night they went down to Grand Case Beach and rented two beach chairs and watched the sun slowly set. Gabriele forgot this was a French territory but was reminded when she saw several swimmers topless. She looked at Dillard, who just smiled and shrugged his shoulders.

"They say, when in Rome . . . ," Dillard said.

"Not on your life, buster," Gabriele replied but turned away to hide the secret smile.

At 10:00 a.m., Hodge showed up in his beat-up taxi. He jumped out and came around to open the door for them.

Dillard introduced Gabriele, and he took her hand, saying, "*Madame, vous êtes vraiment belle.*"

When they were in the car, Gabriele whispered, "What did he say?"

Chapter 61

Hodge lived up to his recommendation. They saw beaches only the locals knew about, drank guavaberry liquor, danced to reggae music, and ate fish caught locally and prepared by the fishermen who caught it. By eleven thirty, they were both exhausted, but Hodge seemed to be going strong.

"Enough, Hodge, we've had enough. Take us home," Gabriele pleaded happily.

Dillard was out on the tiny dance floor with a dark-skinned woman in a colorful madras dress who was holding him close from behind, saying, "Feel the beat, feel the beat." They were both laughing hysterically, and the fact that the woman outweighed him by a good hundred pounds gave her pretty good control. Gabriele loved it. She had already had her turn dancing with the dark-skinned woman. The music stopped, but the two dancers were still laughing. Finally, Dillard headed back to their table, wiping the tears from his eyes.

"You looked pretty good out there, mon," Hodge said grinning.

"How could you tell where I left off and she began?" Dillard said laughing. The European travelers were right; this was a night they wouldn't forget.

Back at the hotel, Dillard paid Hodge a large tip. He had earned every penny and had fun doing it.

"So what you do tomorrow, mon?" Hodge asked.

Dillard thought he was looking for another gig.

"We're going to rent a scooter and go into the rain forest." *What do you think?* he thought for a moment.

"Good plan, but you need a guide."

"Well, we weren't really going to hire anyone to take us," he said.

"No, mon, not saying hire a guide, I guide you for free. I have scooter and am free tomorrow."

Dillard thought for a moment. "Okay," he said. "Come with us then. We'll cruise around and then have lunch somewhere. I'm picking up the scooter at 9:00 a.m., so if you want to meet us here at ten o'clock, we'll head out."

Hodge nodded his head yes and turned to leave.

Back in the hotel room, they got ready for bed. Dillard was in the bathroom brushing his teeth, and when he came out, Gabriele was already curled up in bed. He thought she was sleeping. He turned out the lamp on the nightstand and turned on his side away from Gabriele. He heard the covers rustling and felt her body move up against his.

"Feel the beat, feel the beat," she said, pressing against him tightly.

Dillard picked up the little Vespa and drove it back to the hotel. Weather was supposed to be sunny, no rain in sight, so the perfect day for a ride into the mountains. He called Gabriele from the house phone, and she said she'd be right down. He reminded her to put the "Do Not Disturb" sign on the door. He heard a noise outside, and Hodge pulled up on an old Yamaha scooter that had seen better days, but it was still running.

"Don't let its looks fool you, mon. It be old but still work good, like me." He grinned and revved the little engine.

Dillard just smiled and shook his head. Gabriele showed up wearing cutoff jeans and a tropical-print blouse. Both men appreciated how she looked.

"So, Dillard, I'm driving, right?" she said, pretending to drive the scooter.

"Uhh, no dear," he said, "that be my job."

She pretended to frown. "Well, okay, but just this once," Gabriele said.

Hodge laughed.

Dillard had read about Rocklin Estate, the adventure park that offered zip lines and chairlift rides up on Sentry Hill. He really wasn't interested in that part of the rain forest; he was really looking for a natural setting. He hoped Hodge might know some trails or roads they could take.

They headed out toward Philippsburg. They turned west at Rambaund and went down to Rue Lotterie. There were many walking paths and trailheads in the area, but some of the trails just led to locked gates and private property. They continued on taking Route de Pic Paradise and turned right down the long hill to Lotterie Farm. All around them birds sang, and the tropical foliage was in full bloom.

Beautiful, Dillard thought, appreciating the green canopy.

When they got to the farm, there was a fee of ten dollars; they paid and got a map. This was for the trails to the top of the hill. Hodge pulled ahead and motioned them to follow him up the service road. About halfway up the road, there was a big piece of granite. Hodge motioned them to stop. They got off the scooters and climbed up on the rock. From there they could see the eastern part of the island stretching below. They got back on the scooters and continued up to the summit. Near the top, they took the left fork where the hiking trail intersected the road. Dillard could see communication towers off to his left, and Hodge took them right to the viewpoint. There they could see the island of Saint Barts and more of the eastern side of the island. There was a hiking trail going off to the south with a sign that said "Flagstaff," which was the highest point on the Dutch side. There were no service roads to it, so after spending an hour taking pictures and looking around, the trio headed back down the road toward Philippsburg.

They drove through the town. There were no cruise ships in port, so it was relatively quiet. Gabriele marveled at the shops lined up on the main street. Shop after shop advertised duty-free shopping for liquor and jewelry. Philippsburg was known for its gold and silver jewelry set with precious gems. Prices were said to be much lower than buying in the United States. They pulled the bikes over to the curb and went up to an open-air bar. They were handed menus, and they drank guavaberry coladas while looking over the food selections. Dillard noticed that lobsters were sold by the pound. He couldn't imagine a lobster tail weighing four pounds, but it was on the menu. Gabriele wanted to know if they could buy guavaberry liquor in the States. Hodge said there was a distributor in Miami. He said they just needed the guavaberry liquor, fresh pineapple juice, and cream of coconut to make a guavaberry colada. Gabriele wrote the ingredients down.

They spent two hours in town, eating and drinking. Gabriele walked the shops while the men stayed at the café and talked. When she came back, they were ready to go back to the hotel.

They dropped Gabriele off at the hotel, then Hodge followed Dillard back to the scooter rental shop. He dropped it off and rode back behind Hodge. At the hotel, they said their goodbyes. Dillard planned to call him in a few days. He walked through the lobby and noticed a few new tourists sitting at the bar and in the lounge area. He pressed the elevator for the third floor, and the doors closed, whisking him upstairs. He removed the "Do Not Disturb" sign and unlocked the door. He could hear the shower running. Putting his room key on the entry table, he turned toward the bedroom. The front room coat closet was open slightly, and he went over to close it. He looked inside and saw his white jacket hanging there. He opened the closet all the way and then turned and rushed into the bathroom to check on Gabriele. He startled her, and when she asked him what was wrong, he said someone had been in their room.

Dillard called downstairs and asked if their room had been made up today. The front desk replied that the cleaning people reported a "Do Not Disturb" sign on the door, so they left it. He thanked them and hung up.

Dillard was a creature of habit when not in a war zone. He always hung his dress coat on the third hanger of a closet and buttoned it. His coat was on the first hanger and was unbuttoned. He took the coat out and started searching it for trackers, but he didn't find anything. Still, he knew they had been compromised somehow. They had flown here under assumed names with credit cards that matched. Neither of them had called out on their cell phones, so how did anyone track them? He needed to call Rossof but didn't want to do it from the room. He went downstairs to the lobby. He sat down in a corner and took his cell phone out. He removed the battery and back case, looking for a listening device. None was there, so he reassembled it and turned it on.

They already knew Dillard and Gabriele were in Saint Martin, so he might as well use the cell phone. He dialed Rossof's private number, and he answered.

"They know we're here," he said without preamble.

To Rossof's credit, he didn't bother asking how he knew. "How secure are you?" was his response.

"Third floor facing east. Windows in bedroom and living room, east side. About four hundred yards to access point." He was referring to a point where a sniper could have a good shot.

Rossof was silent for thirty seconds. "Four hours for security detail to arrive. Go to ground." The phone clicked off.

Dillard put the iPhone in airplane mode. He went back upstairs and into the room. Closing the drapes, he went into the bedroom and closed those also. Gabriele was still in the bathroom. Dillard started packing their things.

Marvin Coss and Greg Abbot got the call. They were CIA resident agents living in Puerto Rico. Marvin at once called the airport and was transferred to a private hangar. The US government kept a *Cessna* Denali single-engine turboprop fueled and ready in case they had to get to one of the Virgin Islands quickly. Saint Martin was less than two hours away in the speedy aircraft. Coss had set the flight in motion, notifying the tower and airport security that they would be leaving without a flight plan. The air traffic controllers were notified. Coss and Abbot packed their equipment and left for the airport fifteen minutes after getting the call.

Dillard went into the bathroom and closed the door. He held his fingers to his lips to warn her not to speak. He went over and turned the shower on full, masking their low voices. He told her what they must do.

Chapter 62

They carried one bag each down the back stairs to the first floor. Dillard carefully looked out of the small door window. He saw the same couple at the bar that he had seen coming in. He noticed their drink glasses were full and the ice had melted. They weren't drinking; they were waiting for someone, and he knew whom. They couldn't go out through the front, and they couldn't stay here. It was just a matter of time until a team went to the room since the drapes were drawn, and the sniper was useless.

Dillard assumed they would have all the exits under surveillance. He thought for a minute then decided to call Hodge. It was risky bringing him into this, but he offered the only quick way to get away from the hotel. He didn't know how the man would react to this situation. It would be dangerous to help them, but Dillard believed he would do it. He made the call.

* * *

The couple at the bar heard the commotion out front of the hotel lobby. They looked at each other, then the man got off the stool and went into the lobby to check it out. The woman stayed at the bar. There was a tremendous crash, then the concierge and two bellhops ran outside and began shouting in French. The man from the bar walked outside, trying to find out what was happening. The woman turned and watched the lobby, trying to see what the man was doing. At the end of the bar, a door opened, and two people came out and walked across to the kitchen. They went through the kitchen door and out the back into a service alley. They kept walking away from the hotel toward Grand Case. Dillard had figured it was an even shot that the back alley wouldn't be watched since the only way to get to it was through the bar or lobby, both under surveillance. The taxi pulled up just in front of them. They hurried to it and got in the back. Hodge took off toward Marigot.

"So what was the distraction? It must have been good because it was loud."

"Strange, really, one of those big snakes—a python, I think—was in the tour bus parked just in front of the hotel. Fortunately, I had my twelve-gage shotgun, so I shot it for them. I guess I'm a hero now." He grinned.

"That is strange, Hodge, since pythons aren't native to Saint Martin."

"So what's next, my friends?"

"We have to lie low for a few hours until help arrives. Hodge, we aren't criminals or anything, and the US government is supporting us." He looked at Hodge, who didn't seem to care.

"No worries, I know just the place to go. Besides, this is kinda fun."

"Glad you think so," Gabriele said, not looking amused.

The bar was certainly not a tourist spot. There were only four stools, and one was taken by a man that must have had a rough night, judging from the snoring sounds. He seemed quite comfortable using the wooden planks of the bar for a pillow. He didn't miss a beat when Dillard, Hodge, and Gabriele came in and sat next to him.

"No one will look for you here, and they have the best conch and dumplings on the island," Hodge said, smacking his lips. Dillard didn't like it, too exposed, and although it was off the tourist path, it wouldn't be hard to find.

"We need to be somewhere out of sight, Hodge," Dillard said. "This won't work." He had already counted over a dozen places a shooter could sit undetected and have a clear shot at the bar. Hodge looked disappointed, but of course, he had no idea who was after them or what their capabilities were.

"What about that building over there?" Dillard asked, pointing to a wooden structure that was used for storing lumber. "Looks like there is room for us inside."

Hodge looked at the shed. "Be right back," he said, and he went inside the little restaurant to ask about the shed.

"They said there are chairs inside that the workers use during breaks. We can go inside. They will bring the food to us."

Dillard didn't know what food he was referring to and decided not to ask. Gabriele and Dillard got up and walked over to the shed. The snoring man never missed a beat.

Inside the shed, piles of two-by-fours lined the racks. There were several drums of tar and roofing shingles stacked in a corner, and against one wall were more sections of lumber and several metal ladders. *Looks like roofing supplies*, Dillard thought.

They pulled three chairs away from the wall under the window. Dillard wanted them sitting in the back of the shed. There were no openings back there, and he had a good view of the door. They set up the chairs, and Dillard closed the door. A few minutes later, the door opened, and a young girl carrying three bowls and their glasses came in. She set the food and drink on the ledge under the window and handed Dillard the bill. He paid it, and she left. Dillard closed the door and propped a board against it. It was hot and dusty in the room, but they would survive.

Dillard sat back in the corner; he wasn't hungry. Gabriele and Hodge dug into the food with gusto. He wanted to think about the last few hours, how they had played out, and what went wrong. He was confused. Dillard wouldn't normally put a civilian in this type of danger, but he did. Hodge didn't deserve this; neither did Gabriele. So why had he used Hodge?

Normally, Dillard would never put Gabriele or himself in harm's way, but in this case, he had let them get trapped with no exit plan. Stupid. He knew better, so why? He had let Gabriele turn him into a tourist, and now she was paying the price. To make it worse, he had asked Hodge to get involved, a man he had only known for a day. Had anyone working for him created this situation, he would have at once removed him or her from the field. But here he was, hoping for rescue and not controlling the situation. This had to change.

Gabriele knew he was upset but didn't know what to do about it. She figured that being responsible for her and Hodge had somehow caused him to not act as he normally would. She had never been in this situation and didn't have a clue how to deal with it. Both she and Hodge were completely dependent on him, and somehow she had to get him back on track. But how? She decided to just approach it directly. She got up and went over to where he was sitting.

"Dillard, I don't know what is going on with you, but Hodge and I have complete faith in you. If you need to do something to protect us, then do it. I don't pretend to know what that is, but obviously, you feel you should be doing more than you are. If that's the case, just get up and do it." He just stared at her.

Dillard made up his mind. He'd worry about how the Russians had known their location later, but right now, there were more important issues. He stood up and kissed Gabriele.

"I need to make a little trip outside. You need to promise me that no matter what you hear, you will stay in here with the door closed until I tell you to come out. Do you promise?"

Hodge was listening.

"I promise, Dillard," she said. Hodge nodded his head yes.

Dillard looked around the shed. It was about twenty feet long and fifteen feet wide, filled with shelves stacked with boards and roofing shingles. There was a window in the back, but the trees had grown up against the cracked glass. Dillard started moving boxes of debris away from the wall with the window. Using a dirty rag, he grabbed one of the broken panes of glass and, wiggling it back and forth, removed it from the frame. He continued on until all the glass was gone. Then he reached out and pushed the thorny bushes away. The small trees, he could bend over out of the way, but the larger-diameter trees, he could only bend a little. It was going to be a tight fit, and painful because of the thorny bushes.

He went over to Gabriele and Hodge.

"I'm going out that window. You are staying here." It wasn't a request, and both knew it. "I'll be gone about two hours. Our friends should be here by then, but do not open this door unless you hear my voice or Rossof's voice." Dillard knew Rossof would come with the team. "Let's brace the door with some of this lumber."

He and Hodge rummaged through the boards and found several two-by-fours to wedge against the door.

"When I leave, I need you and Gabriele to sit over there, away from the door." He pointed to a corner. "The closer to the floor, the better." Gabriele didn't look thrilled about sitting with the spiders and ants that had already staked a claim on that section of the shed.

"Okay, let's get going." Dillard walked over to the window in the back and started climbing out through the bushes. No one asked him where he was going.

Chapter 63

Dillard tried to keep the noise down. Trying to crawl over and through the small trees and bushes was a nightmare. After ten feet of fighting his way through the tangled mess, his shirt was shredded from the thorns, as were his face and hands. His legs had fared better because his pants were thicker. Most of the time, he was on his hands and knees. He put the discomfort aside, focusing his mind on the goal.

The bushes and brush had thinned out behind the bar, and he was able to make better time. He still had to crawl; he didn't want to be seen. Dillard didn't know if anyone was out in the trees by the access road, but he was done leaving things to chance. He might lose a little blood and find that no one was out there, and that would be okay. Sitting in the shed hoping to be rescued was not okay.

He had come to an area of about fifty yards from the spot he would have chosen if he was the sniper. He would have to go farther down in the bushes alongside the road to cross the open space to that side of the trees. He kept working through the bushes until he was well out of sight of the assumed sniper spot. He stood up, his head about two feet above the thorny bushes, and pushed his way onto the road. He saw no parked vehicles, so maybe he was wrong.

Only one way to find out, he thought.

The tree side of the road was much clearer of brush than the way he had come, and travel was fairly easy. Everything was wet from humidity and rain, so he was able to move quietly. He moved from tree to tree, never exposing himself to where the shooters might be. He was within twenty yards of the spot when he smelled cigarette smoke. He had heard and seen nothing. He dropped to the ground and lay still, searching ahead. Still no sign of him or them. He lay there about ten minutes, ignoring his new best friends that crawled up his pants and feasted on his bloody skin.

There! Movement, he thought, focusing on a darker shade of green some twenty yards away. He saw the dark-green patch move just slightly. That was enough.

Dillard figured he could get close enough to the dark-green spot without being spotted. The question in his mind was whether Green Spot was alone or not. He doubted it. He watched for a while longer then decided to move over to the right of Green Spot, thinking that if there was another man there, he would be on the roadside. Again, all this planning was based on what he would do in this situation.

He almost fell flat on his face, tripping on one of the sucker vines snaking down from a tamarind tree. He caught himself just in time and froze. Nothing had changed over at Green Spot, and now he could see an outline of a body and glow from a cigarette. Maybe that was why Dillard never started smoking. He looked around and saw a line of manchineel trees, thorny bushes, and a huge kapok tree within ten feet of Green Spot. If he approached using the kapok to block Green Spot's view, he could get close enough to attack him. He didn't have a plan for the other man if he was there. He knew to stay away from the manchineel trees because the sap was toxic.

He quickly reached the kapok tree, still hoping to learn if the shooter was alone. Then he heard a low-pitched voice say something quietly and a higher-pitched voice answer. Now he knew. He looked around for a weapon. The jungle floor was littered with branches, and he saw one about two inches thick. It was a little long for a club, but it would do. He bent down to pick it up, and when he did, the second man saw him. He yelled to the shooter and jumped up to bring his pistol to bear, but Dillard had launched himself as soon as the man saw him. The second man's arm was almost around to point the gun at him, but Dillard's foot caught him under the chin. The gun went flying, and he fell back into the manchineel trees. Dillard quickly whipped around and saw the rifle coming to bear. He dived under the muzzle and grabbed the shooter's ankles and yanked hard. The rifle went off, putting four ascending holes in the kapok tree, as Dillard grabbed the rifle and kneed the shooter in the face. Blood shot out of his smashed nose and lips, and Dillard was able to rip the rifle from his hands and club him with the gunstock. He stopped moving. Dillard quickly turned just as the second man charged. Dillard shot him in the heart. Both men were down.

He went over to the dead man and removed his belt, then he took his off. Green Spot was quickly lashed to a small tree with the belts. Then Dillard removed the belt from the unconscious man and looped it under his chin and fastened it around the tree. He was now secured by his arms and neck.

Dillard walked out to the road and then started back to the shed. When he got to the door, he knocked and called Gabriele's name. He could hear the boards being removed from the door, and it finally opened. Both Gabriele and Hodge just stared at him for a few seconds, then Gabriele jumped into his arms, crying.

"Hey, kiddo, I'm fine, and we're going to be okay," Dillard said into her hair.

"You sure don't look fine," she said, still crying. Hodge just stood there, looking at him.

Rossof and his men got there forty-five minutes later. Dillard had seen his reflection in a broken mirror, and he understood why Gabriele said he didn't look fine. It was all superficial, though, and it would heal quickly. Until then, he would look like roadkill, but he could live with that.

One of Rossof's men was a field medic and cleaned Dillard up as best he could. He gave him several small tubes of salve for the cuts and scrapes, which were already beginning to itch. Dillard asked Hodge and Gabriele to wait by the shed for a minute, and he walked down the road to where Rossof and his men were talking to the shooter, who was now awake. They had wiped his face with a damp cloth and given him water. That was the end of the pleasantries. They grilled him mercilessly until they had all they were going to get. Rossof had some leads he would follow when they got back. He called the transport driver and told him to come pick them up. He had dropped them off a quarter of a mile from the shed.

The van pulled up, and they loaded the prisoner into the back. Gabriele and Hodge got in the first seats; the soldiers and Dillard sat in the next two rows. Rossof was in the front next to the driver. Nobody was talking.

They drove to the Grand Case Airport where Rossof had landed. They went through security and were allowed to drive to one of the support hangars away from the terminal. Rossof's Cessna was parked there. Everyone got out of the van, and Dillard was given a US Army shirt to replace his rags. Gabriele gasped when she saw the cuts and welts covering his chest, arms, and back. He looked at her and shrugged then put the shirt on as if nothing was wrong.

Rossof had one of the soldiers take the shooter into the plane first, securing him in the rear seat. Dillard turned to Hodge.

"They're going to take you back to the hotel," he said. "Is there going to be trouble because of the snake and shotgun?"

"I don't think I will do too much business with *Hotel L'Esplanade.*" He smiled sadly.

"Oh, I think we can fix that," Rossof said smiling. "And I hope you like the new Yamaha scooter they left there for you. Here are the keys." He handed Hodge a pair of Yamaha keys, shook his hand, and walked away toward the Cessna, talking on his cell phone.

"Thank you for everything, my friend, and someday I hope Gabriele and I can come see you again."

They shook hands, and Hodge pulled him into a short hug.

"Please leave the men with guns home next time." He grinned happily and pulled Gabriele into a hug; only it wasn't as short as Dillard's hug.

When she could catch her breath, she told him that if he ever came to the States, he would be their guest. He smiled at that, waved, and started walking to the van that would take him to the hotel. Dillard and Gabriele turned and walked to the boarding ladder of the Cessna.

When Hodge got to the hotel, the manager and concierge came rushing out.

"Monsieur Hodge, we are so happy you are back," the manager gushed. "The governor told us how you risked your own life and rescued that poor American and his wife. She said she would make sure all the tourist offices know of how brave and honest you are. And of course, it will surely mean a boost in tourists visiting our hotel, since from now on, you are the only tour guide we will recommend. And if you would like to use the Mercedes van, it is at your disposal." He smiled again.

"What about Pierre?" Hodge said. "I thought he always used it for your tourists."

"Pierre no longer works with us. We want you to be our exclusive guide, and of course, we will pay all expenses."

Chapter 64

Even after two weeks, Dillard's body was still a mass of cuts. He was pumped full of antibiotics to fight infections, and he had creams and lotions, but time was the only true healer. The itching had stopped now, and the wounds no longer wept, so they were just ugly. He didn't take his shirt off in public, and in a week or two, they should be pretty much gone. Gabriele had gotten used to it and was no longer afraid to touch him. He had to admit he looked like a leper when they first got back. His face was so scratched up and swollen that he was almost unrecognizable.

He hadn't heard from Rossof for several weeks. He didn't know what had happened with the prisoner; hopefully, they were able to figure out who was passing on the information.

Gabriele came in from swimming in the lake. She was spending a lot of time at Dillard's house. They talked about combining their lives. Dillard had never considered marriage, but it seemed to be their direction. They were already making plans to sell her house. Her job had been the only issue, but she learned that she could transfer to Santa Fe College near the house, so that issue was resolved. She loved the lake house. Her kids promised to visit regularly, but she figured she'd be doing a lot of the visiting, not them. But was Dillard really ready for this? He'd been on his own for so many years, but somehow they just seemed to mesh. He was smart enough not to go forward with this idea if it didn't work for him.

Dillard sat in his study thinking about Saint Martin. The whole scenario just didn't seem right, and he couldn't pinpoint what was bothering him. He didn't like that Rossof hadn't called him about the prisoner or, for that matter, updated him on Yari. Maybe he was just being suspicious, but then, that's why he was still around. His cell phone rang.

"Sorry for the absence, Master Chief, I've been busy," was how Rossof started the conversation.

"Tell me about the prisoner," Dillard said.

"No luck with him. In fact, I got word that he died from his injuries. I guess you hit him harder than we thought."

Dillard was puzzled. The prisoner was coherent and talking when they left Saint Martin. He didn't say anything.

"You're probably wondering about Yari also. He is going to be moved to a safe location because of the continued Russian threat. I can't disclose where he's going, but he'll be kept under wraps."

Again, Dillard didn't say anything. Then he said, "So no idea on how the Russians learned about Saint Martin?"

"Well, the theory is that they somehow tracked you by cell phone."

"I guess that's possible," was all Dillard said. "Can I talk to Yari before he leaves? He still in Alexandria?"

Rossof cleared his throat before he answered, "I'll put in the request, but no promises. They're really keeping him under wraps."

"I'd appreciate it, Captain."

"You take care, and I'll update you on Yari." He disconnected.

Gabriele walked into the study, still wearing her two-piece swimsuit. He looked at her then looked again. She knew that look.

"Forget it, buster. Dinner comes first, then we'll see." She laughed at his disappointed look. "Was that Rossof? How's he doing?"

"He sounds fine. The prisoner was a dead end [he didn't say why], and Yari is going to be moved to a safer location somewhere."

"I hope Yari's okay. Did you know Yari and Emily have been talking to each other?"

"No, I'm surprised that they let him call her."

"I don't think they know."

Dillard's eyebrows raised. "Sneaky bastard."

Dinner and the rest went fine. Still, Dillard was troubled. He decided he needed to see Yari but wasn't sure how to approach it with Rossof. He had made it clear that Yari was locked down; still, he wanted to talk to him. He brought the subject up with Gabriele that night.

"Why is it so important to see Yari, Dillard?"

"I'm not really sure, but I feel it's important. I just have to figure out how to do it. Do you think Emily would help me?"

"I'm sure she would like to, but I don't know how she could help."

"How about we spend a couple of days in St. Augustine, visit with the kids?"

"You know I'd love that."

The next day, Dillard and Gabriele packed up for a few days at her house in St. Augustine. Dillard locked up and set up the alarm system that he had installed after the assassination attempt. He came out to the Jeep, which was already running with the AC on. Gabriele was sitting in the passenger seat, talking to Emily.

"Emily says she'll be at her apartment around six. I said we'd bring dinner."

"Works for me," Dillard said and backed the Jeep up the driveway to the road.

They headed off for St. Augustine, about an hour's drive from his house. On the road, they talked a little about selling her house, what to do with the money, and how to stay connected to her kids and grandchild. Outside traffic was light since most people were at work.

They turned at Green Cove Springs then left at the signal. Dillard liked driving by the old WWII shipyards and boat storage. There were hundreds of sailboats and powerboats up on stands that people were either storing or hoping to forget. Dillard would love to walk around in the storage yard and look at them. Maybe he would one of these days. They passed Shands Pier, where he and Gabriele sometimes launched the Four Winns, then off across Shands Bridge.

Down the road they passed Trout Creek, a private boat ramp and store open to the public. Dillard usually launched the boat in Trout Creek at the county ramp across the private boat ramp. He liked to go up Trout Creek because it was the essence of Florida. The creek was about two hundred feet wide, plenty of room for boats and a popular kayak spot. It was like going back in time up the creek. Oak trees, cypress, and ferns lined the banks, and Spanish moss hung from the branches. You might even see an alligator, but that was rare because they were mostly small and shy around that area. Dillard swore he thought he could hear banjo music playing back in the bogs.

They got to St. Augustine around 4:00 p.m. He unloaded the Jeep while Gabriele went inside to turn the AC up. It was in the low nineties outside, which was hot. He locked the Jeep and came inside. It felt good, and although she usually set the temperature a little too cold for his taste, he said nothing. She handed him an iced tea, and he took it into her living room and sat down on the sofa. She came in a short time later with her drink.

"Okay, so tell me why you are worried about Yari."

He looked at her with appreciation. How did she know something was bothering him? She would have made a good agent.

"I don't know, Gabriele. Some things just aren't adding up. I want to make sure he is all right." She just looked at him.

They got to Emily's apartment a little after six. She was home and had changed from work, so they all sat down in her little living room. Dillard forgot how pretty she was, a young version of his lovely Gabriele. No wonder Yari was infatuated. The two women made small talk about work and home, then Dillard jumped in.

"When was the last time you spoke with Yari?" he said.

She looked surprised. "Well, uh, he called me two nights ago," she said, looking embarrassed.

"How did he sound? Did he talk about leaving the place they're keeping him in?"

"He sounded fine, Dillard, and he didn't say anything about leaving. Why?"

"Well, I just heard that they might be moving him to a safer place."

"He would have told me," she said decisively.

"Yes, I'm sure he would. They probably haven't told him yet." He was silent for a minute. "Em, do you know where they are keeping Yari?" He knew it was a secret, but Yari probably thought it didn't apply to her.

She didn't answer right away but said, "Yes, I know where he's at. Is something wrong?" She started to look upset.

"I doubt it, but I'm thinking of taking a trip to Virginia to see him."

Emily still looked upset. "I'll tell you if you take me with you," she said firmly. "If he is in some kind of trouble, I want to be there."

That was the last thing Dillard needed. He was still mad at himself for putting Hodge and Gabriele in harm's way, and he wasn't about to do it again.

"I'm sorry, Em, that isn't possible. If there is something wrong, I need to be free to act as I see fit. You would only be making it harder."

"I understand, Dillard, but if you want my help, you have to take it all or nothing." She got up off the sofa and went into the kitchen.

Gabriele went after her. The two women talked for about half an hour, then Gabriele came back to the living room. Dillard was still sitting where they had left him. This time it was Gabriele's turn.

"I know you still blame yourself for what happened in Saint Martin, and I can't change that. But the deal is that even with what happened to us, I'm glad I was there." She stared at him.

"Dillard, you don't understand how hard it is to sit at home when the one you care about is somewhere out there where he could get hurt or even killed. I died a little each time the telephone rang, terrified that it's someone calling me to say you're not coming home. I would always rather be by your side than waiting for a phone call, and Emily feels the same way. I don't know how serious this thing is between them, but I do understand what she means when she says she won't be left behind. Neither will I." He didn't know what to say, so he just said how he felt.

"I will die if something happens to you. Same goes for Emily. I let my feelings get in the way of doing my job in Saint Martin, and I can't let that happen again." He paused, knowing that there was nothing he could say to change their minds. "There will be ground rules, rules that will keep you safe and let me do what I need to do. Is that clear?"

She put her hand on his arm. "I will do whatever you tell me to do, and Em will do the same."

"I promise, Dillard," Emily said from the kitchen doorway.

He just shook his head and sighed.

Chapter 65

The JetBlue flight landed at Washington Regan International Airport (DCA) at 10:00 a.m. Dillard had called ahead and rented a car from Enterprise, so they went into the terminal and then over to the rental car service desk. He took the extra insurance, not sure if it would cover bullet holes, but better safe than sorry. They walked outside and found the row and the spot the Ford was parked in. It was a Taurus, so there was plenty of metal around his precious cargo. They stowed their bags then headed out of the airport and across the bridge to Arlington, Virginia. Emily had said the safe house was in Arlington, and Dillard had called an ex-Navy buddy who went into government service when he left the Navy.

Greg Abbot was shocked to hear from Dillard. It had been a good twenty years, and Greg was a year older than Dillard, so he must be close to retirement age. The department he was in retired you at sixty-five regardless of whether you wanted to or not. Somehow he couldn't picture Greg behind a desk, not the Greg Abbot he had served with.

Greg got past his shock quickly, understanding the urgency of Dillard's call. He knew a little about Dillard's actions on behalf of the US government, so the request, although it was outside channels, was something he would do for his old friend. Greg said he'd call him back in five.

Dillard waited in the car while the girls checked into the hotel. Greg called back as promised.

"Something's going on, Dillard. The duty officer in charge of Yari's safe house didn't come to work yesterday or today, and they're having trouble locating him. The Secret Service doesn't misplace their people."

"Did you get the location?"

"Yes, he's at 2214 Losmier Drive in Arlington. There is a car out front with two agents on twenty-four-hour rotations. John Tippins is the acting DO, and he said he'd call the agents and alert them that you were coming by. You must have some major clout to be granted access to Yari. I told him not to alert anyone except the two on-site agents about you coming,"

"Thanks, Greg. I owe you big-time."

"Hey, Dillard, why don't we . . ." He stopped talking because the line was dead.

Dillard typed in the address in the car's GPS. He was only eleven minutes from the house, not counting traffic. DC was impossible to drive in; Alexandria was just as difficult. He added another ten minutes to the drive. Picking up the burner phone, he called Gabriele and told her he'd be gone for a few hours. She didn't ask questions.

He drove out of the hotel parking lot and headed east on Alhambra Avenue then turned left on Old Dominion Boulevard. Two miles later, he turned onto Losmier Drive and started looking for 2214. It was a nice subdivision, the homes upper middle class. It was a typical "hide in plain sight" safe house. He saw the driveway up ahead and a late-model Chevy Blazer parked in front. He could see two heads through the rear glass. Dillard pulled in behind them and parked, getting out of his car slowly with his hands in plain sight. He walked up to the driver's side window, which was rolled down.

"I'm Dillard Ross. I believe John Tippins called about me?"

The driver asked for his ID. Dillard noticed he used only his left hand to take the document; his right hand was probably holding a service weapon.

"I'm Agent Max Lister. This is Agent Rogers. We've heard a lot about you, Mr. Ross, and it's a pleasure to meet you." His hands remained inside the car.

"We can give you thirty minutes with Yari. Will that suffice?"

"That's fine, and I appreciate your cooperation." The conversation was over, and the driver rolled up his window.

Yari met him at the door. He had been alerted that Dillard was stopping by and was surprised and pleased.

"Please come in, my friend," he said enthusiastically, pumping Dillard's hand. "You have cold beer with me, yes?"

"Yes," Dillard answered, moving away from the front door. "Grab the beers, and we'll sit and talk."

Yari happily went into the kitchen to get the drinks. Dillard sat down on the sectional couch, looking around. *Very nice,* he thought, admiring the artwork and furniture.

"Beers for the boys," Yari said, coming in from the kitchen.

Dillard took his beer and decided to jump right in about his concerns.

"Listen, Yari, this isn't just a social visit. I have some questions for you, and you need to listen seriously." His smile disappeared. "Has anything different been happening around here lately?"

Yuri thought a moment. "No, no, I don't think so," he said. "They did change my security guys a few days ago, but that's all I can think of."

"What happened to your previous guards?" Dillard asked.

"Well, I supposed they were transferred to some other job. These new guys are pretty nice. They give me more freedom than the first team. Why?"

"I heard you might be moving to a different location. Have you heard anything about that?"

"No, and I think they would tell me so I can pack and be ready. Is there a new problem?"

"Not that I'm aware of. Something just doesn't feel right. Here's what I'd like to do."

They talked for another fifteen minutes, and Dillard got up to leave.

"By the way, Gabriele and Emily came with me and are staying at the Four Seasons. I know you want to see Em, but don't tell anyone that they are here. Promise me."

Now Yuri looked concerned. "Of course, Dillard.

Chapter 66

Dillard returned to the hotel and told the two women that Yuri was fine. Emily was anxious to see him, but Dillard said she had to wait a bit. He went out on the balcony to think.

He had left Yuri with a simple plan; Yuri was about to be kidnapped. Dillard had looked through the house and found several ways that he could get Yari out without alerting the two security guards. Dillard didn't know what other security measures they had put in place, but he was about to find out. He planned to come back after dark.

He went back inside the hotel room and told the girls they needed to get packed to leave. The urgency of his request made them hold their questions. He then called Greg and asked for another favor. He could tell Greg didn't like this one, but he said he would do it. Dillard said he'd drop by at about four thirty, and Greg said to meet him at the west parking lot just outside the commissary. They hung up. Even though it was a government office building, there were no gates or guards to worry about.

Both women were in the car, and Dillard checked out of the hotel. He got into the driver's seat and headed for Greg's office. He pulled into the entrance and turned left toward the commissary. It was clearly marked. He parked in the second row of cars and waited. A few minutes later, he saw Greg coming out of the building with a duffel bag. He walked up to Dillard's open window and handed him the bag. He put it on the front passenger seat. They shook hands, and Greg turned around and headed back into the building. The exchange took less than five minutes.

"I'm not going to ask what is in the bag and why you need it," Gabriele said from the back seat.

"Good," was all Dillard said.

He pulled out of the parking lot and back onto Old Dominion Road and headed for Yari's safe house. This time he parked one street up on

Wilcox Drive, pulling into the driveway of a house that was for sale. It was a Spanish-style architecture and had a low block wall that separated the curving driveway from the street. While it didn't completely hide the car, it would work unless someone was actually looking for them. He had seen the house when he left Yari's earlier and had called the real estate broker listed on the sign. He verified that the house was vacant. Dillard set up a tour of the house for the following day.

It was just turning 6:00 p.m., and the sun was slowly going down. There was little traffic on Wilcox Drive, just people coming home from work. They shouldn't draw any attention. He turned to face the women in the back.

"Something is wrong. Yari doesn't know anything about being moved, his security has just been changed, and I have a bad feeling. I'm going to get Yari out of the house, and he's coming with us. If I'm wrong, I'll take the heat. I had a friend rent us a cabin in Maryland under an assumed name, and until I find out what is going on, we'll stay there." He turned back around.

"But you don't know for sure that he is in any danger?" Emily asked, concern in her voice.

"No, and I want to be wrong, but just to be safe, he's coming with us. His security is too light if it's only those two security agents. It's more like they're there more to keep him in than keep someone out. Before the guards were changed, they had at least two teams watching the house. Now there's only one."

They sat and waited, making small talk. Dillard opened the bag on the front seat and took out the Glock 40 and spare magazine. At 7:00 p.m., Dillard opened the door of the car. He had turned off the dome light, so nothing showed to alert anyone. The commuter traffic had pretty much stopped, so he got out, putting the gun in the waistband of his pants in the back. He pulled his shirt over it. The extra magazine went into his front pocket.

"Stay in the car. I'll be right back," he told Gabriele.

He looked over the block fence, searching both ways. There were no parked cars on the street, so he headed across and walked east toward the corner of Monroe then left toward Losmier Drive. Just before he got to Yari's Street, he walked across the grass to the fence of the house on the corner. He looked around the fence and could see the security car parked three houses down in front of Yari's house. He had checked earlier to see if his two neighbors had dogs, and it looked like only one family had one.

It was small, probably a house dog, and Dillard hoped it would be inside when he started for Yari's house. None of the houses had back fences, so he was probably right. He was going to approach through the backyards.

The corner house had the backyard light on. Good, it meant it wasn't motion-sensing, and he could stay in the shadows. The next yard was dark, as was Yari's. He was a little concerned about that. While the dark was good, it might mean motion sensors, which would turn on the light if it saw movement. He'd try to stay out of range. There was a divider chain-link fence and small trees down at the bottom end of the yards separating the houses on Wilcox from Losmier. Dillard crept along the fence line, trying to stay out of range of any motion sensors. He made it to Yari's back door and, taking the Glock out of his belt, knocked quietly on the door. It opened immediately; no lights on in the kitchen or hallway, only the living room. Dillard stepped in.

"He said you might show up tonight," a voice said from the gloom.

Dillard heard a gun slide ratchet and knew he was trapped. He could barely make out the speaker, who was being careful not to present a good target.

"I know you're armed, so lose the piece."

Dillard had no option but to do as told. "Where's Yari?" he said to the shadow.

"Oh, don't worry, you two will be reunited soon."

Dillard could hear the cold confidence in the shadow's voice. He recognized him as Agent Lister; the other security guy must be in the other room providing backup.

"We're coming out. Keep your eyes on him," he said to backup. "Move into the living room, Mr. Ross. You can try something if you like. We don't mind." Again, the cold, confident voice. Dillard liked that; confidence was always a great tool for him to use.

"Okay, I won't try anything," he said, starting to move toward the living room. It got brighter as he got closer. Dillard could see Lister standing by the refrigerator, and the silenced 9 mm in his hand was tracking him. He needed to see where the other agent was before he could do anything. Meekly he kept walking into the lighted room.

Yari was sitting on the sofa by the windows. The drapes had been drawn. He looked up at Dillard, blood trickling down from the gash on his forehead. *Pistol-whipped*, Dillard thought. He walked into the center of the room and stopped.

"Call R," Lister told Rogers. Rogers got out his cell phone and dialed.

"Empty your pockets, Ross," Lister said, motioning with his pistol for Dillard to put the contents on the coffee table near his legs.

Dillard took out the change and car keys and put them on the table. From the other pocket, he took out his cell phone and the extra magazine. His wallet came next. When he was done, Lister motioned him to go stand near Yari. Dillard did as he was instructed.

"Okay, both," Rogers said in Russian.

That answered one of the questions Dillard had. Rogers put the cell phone away and spoke to Lister in Russian. Lister nodded and told him to tie wrap Dillard's wrists. He had noticed that Yari was already secured.

Rogers moved over to Dillard, being careful to stay out of the way of Lister's gun. Dillard knew that if he made any sudden moves, Lister would shoot him before he could do anything. Rogers took out two thick tie wraps and told Dillard to put out his wrists.

Just as he did, a loud voice said, "Put your guns down now."

Lister swung around, looking for the voice, just as Dillard struck Rogers with his palm heel, driving his jaw up and snapping his neck back. Then he grabbed Rogers's wrist above the hand with the gun. Dillard twisted it savagely, and Rogers screamed as bones cracked. Dillard spun him around to face Lister holding the arm with the shattered wrist under his armpit. He pulled Rogers's finger back, which was still on the trigger, and Lister went down with three holes in his chest. Dillard ripped the gun from Rogers's hand and kicked his legs out from under him. Rogers hit the ground, still screaming and holding his wrist.

Yari looked stunned. It had all happened so fast he wasn't even sure what had just taken place. Dillard walked over to Lister lying on the floor and kicked his gun away. Then he picked up his cell phone from the coffee table, turning off the alarm that he had set. Had nothing happened when he came into Yari's house, he would have disabled the alarm that was programmed with his voice yelling "Put your guns down now!" over and over.

They went out the front door, not bothering to stay hidden. Dillard knew only two agents were watching Yari, and they were both incapacitated. He had left Rogers tied to the water heater in the closet. Dillard called Greg and told him what had happened. He asked him not to report it yet; he didn't want to alert whoever was controlling the two agents. Greg agreed and said he would have one of his men go to the safe house to pick Rogers up. Lister could stay where he was for now.

Yari and Dillard walked back to the car. Emily saw them coming and ran out onto the street, wrapping her arms around Yari. *So much for security,* Dillard thought. Gabriele was standing by the driver's door, waiting for Dillard to approach. Then she too wrapped her arms around Dillard.

They drove to the rental house in Maryland. Once inside, the four sat on the couch talking about what had happened. Yari wanted to know how Dillard had found out about the plot to kill him and Dillard, but all he would say was that something just didn't feel right. That made no sense to Yari, but Gabriele shook her head like she understood. They talked about what to do next, and Dillard said he had to find out who was pulling the strings. Gabriele wanted to know if he had called Captain Rossof, and he said, "No, not yet."

Gabriele and Dillard went out to the car. They were going to pick up some food, but it was more than just to give Emily and Yari some private time. They took their time, driving around White Oak Shopping Center on New Hampshire Avenue. There were a dozen of fast-food and sit-down eateries that could provide takeout, and Gabriele picked Woo's Chinese Restaurant because they stayed open until 11:00 p.m. She called in the order, and they drove around Silver Springs while they waited for the food to be ready. Back at the shopping center, Dillard went into the restaurant and picked up the food. He put it in the back seat of the car and started back to the rental house.

* * *

"Mne net dela do bespokoystva Moskvy, ya spravlyus!" he shouted into the cell phone then abruptly disconnected the line. (I don't care about Moscow's concerns, I'll handle it!)

The man was angry—angry that Moscow would question his actions and angry that his two agents had failed. While he didn't accept responsibility for their failure, he should have known that Dillard Ross would come up with something to turn the tables. Privately he admitted he should have planned better, but these agents were supposed to be the best. Well, they had certainly met their match.

Angry as he was, he had to admit that Dillard Ross had lived up to his reputation. He stuffed the miniature micro flash drive from his safe into the tiny lead-lined pocket of his shirt cuff. The computer was already wiped, as were his cell phone calls. It was well past work hours, but the building security was used to people working at all hours, so his being in the office so late wasn't unusual. He picked up the valise and headed out of his office, going downstairs to the first floor.

The duty officer checked the contents of his valise, but he only found normal department communication printouts. Next the man went through the x-ray machine, but it saw nothing. There were no metal parts in the micro flash drive, and the lead pocket was small and placed in a spot that was unobtrusive. When he crossed his arms above his head, it was almost invisible to the machine. He collected his valise and headed out the door, saying good night to the security guards and duty officer. He knew he wouldn't be back.

Outside he went toward his dedicated parking spot with his name sign proudly proclaiming his importance. He unlocked the government Blazer and threw his valise into the front passenger seat. He got in and closed the door. A dark figure in the back seat spoke to him in Russian, startling him.

"*Ya ne budu sprashivat', zachem ty eto sdelal, my vo vsem razberemsya pozzhe,*" the dark figure said. (I won't ask why you did it. We'll figure all that out later.)

He looked in the rearview mirror at the dark figure.

In English, the dark figure said, "Unfortunately, Captain, you won't be around to see the results." The suppressed Ruger spit death into Captain Rossof's brain.

Chapter 67

They sat on the screened porch, watching the sun reflect rainbows on the lake. Both were quiet. Gabriele took Dillard's hand.

"I'm so sorry about Captain Rossof, Dillard. It's so hard to believe that a stupid drunk driver killed such a wonderful man. Are you planning to go to the funeral ceremony? I heard that several countries are sending emissaries to attend. Captain Rossof was a great man, and I know he was your friend." A tear slid down her cheek, and Dillard turned and looked at her.

"Would you like to go?" he said. "We could drive upstate afterward and see Emily and Yari—I mean, Emily and Peter."

Gabriele chuckled. "I'd like that. She sounds really happy, Dillard, and we haven't seen them since the wedding. Em says Peter really likes his job and he is happy, even after learning about the death of his father."

"I'd like that too, honey, and besides, I think we deserve a little break."

"Break from what?" Gabriele said smiling. "You're retired, and my job is fun, so it's not like we have a lot of stress to shed." She laughed.

"Okay, it's decided then. We'll drive to DC, pay our respects at the funeral ceremony, then motor up to Pennsylvania, and see the kids." He stood up, stretching.

His cell phone rang, and he picked it up, looking at the caller ID. He recognized Greg's number.

"This is Ross," he said, answering, "and this had better be good."

Greg's voice came on the line. "Chief, have you ever heard of a place called the Kuril Islands?"

The End

3 Marbles

Paperback ISBN-13: 978-1956823172
eBook ISBN-13: 978-1956823981

In 1999, a terrified three-year-old hides and listens while his neighbors are being murdered. Soon after, the young boy escapes from Chilapa, Mexico with his parents under the wooden bed of an old truck. Arriving illegally in El Paso that night, his father gives Alex three marbles saying that they are very important and that someday he would understand why. That same night, his father disappears.

At age five, Alex doesn't yet understand his environment. At age six, his mother dies, and he is left on his own. At age seven, Alex learns how to hide from the older street boys who beat him for sport and at age nine, Alex stops hiding.

Julia lives with a group of orphaned kids on the streets of El Paso. She is curious about Alex because he's a loner and acts different than the other kids she knows. Julia is in the basement the day Brian, Randy, and Eric corner the smaller boy and decide to give him a beating. After witnessing what Alex does to the older boys, Julia becomes afraid of him and vows keeps her distance. Now, three years later, Julia again meets up with Alex. Although they have had little interaction over the years, they both realize that some type of bond exists between them, even if they don't understand what It Is.

This is the story of a Hispanic boy and girl; forgotten children growing up together in a world with no welcome mat. Preyed upon by drug dealers, immigration agents and their own peers, Alex and Julia find a way to survive and finally leave the streets of old El Paso.

About the Author
Jan R. McDonald

Businessman, Author, and World Traveler, Jan R McDonald is a natural born storyteller.

From bedtime stories to monthly newsletters to his grandchildren, Mr. McDonald combines real life experiences with fictional situations that create entertaining and absorbing reads.

Retired and now living in Florida, Jan R. McDonald has borrowed from his real-life experiences to create humorous, fictional and non-fiction adventures.

Another fiction work by Mr. McDonald is *3 Marbles* which was published in 2022.